THE LIZARD BEAT

The movie was so good that I forgot all about how scary it was and that I was all alone in the middle of the night. Until it was over, that is. Then I thought about the dreams I was going to have, and all of a sudden I felt a cold chill.

I was almost to the point of running into the kitchen and looking up the number of the resort where Mom and Dad were staying, when the lizards came onto the screen. These were real lizards, not people dressed up as lizards, and they played regular musical instruments. At first it was scarier than the movie, especially the close-ups. The music sounded funny at first, but I got used to it very fast, and then I liked it more than anything I'd ever heard.

LIZARD MUSIC

"Imaginative and appealing. A shoo-in for awards and for popularity among readers, young and old."
—*PUBLISHERS WEEKLY*

BANANA TWIST by Florence Parry Heide

BE A PERFECT PERSON IN JUST THREE DAYS!
by Stephen Manes

BONES ON BLACK SPRUCE MOUNTAIN
by David Budbill

THE CASTLE IN THE ATTIC
by Elizabeth Winthrop

THE CHOCOLATE TOUCH
by Patrick Skene Catling

CHRISTOPHER by Richard M. Koff

C.L.U.T.Z by Marilyn Z. Wilkes

THE CURSE OF THE BLUE FIGURINE
by John Bellairs

HOW I KEPT THE U.S. OUT OF WAR by Judi Miller

JOHN MIDAS IN THE DREAMTIME
by Patrick Skene Catling

THE MUFFIN FIEND by Daniel Pinkwater

NUTTY FOR PRESIDENT by Dean Hughes

SNOWSHOE TREK TO OTTER RIVER
by David Budbill

LIZARD MUSIC

D. MANUS PINKWATER

A BANTAM SKYLARK BOOK®
TORONTO · NEW YORK · LONDON · SYDNEY · AUCKLAND

RL 5, 009-012

This edition contains the complete text
of the original hardcover edition.
NOT ONE WORD HAS BEEN OMITTED.

LIZARD MUSIC

A Bantam Book / published by arrangement with Dodd, Mead &
Company, Inc.

PRINTING HISTORY

Dodd, Mead edition published 1976

Bantam Skylark edition / June 1988

Skylark Books is a registered trademark of Bantam Books, a
division of Bantam Doubleday Dell Publishing Group, Inc.
Registered in the U.S. Patent and Trademark Office and elsewhere.

ISBN 0-553-15605-5

Published simultaneously in the United States and Canada

Bantam Books are published by Bantam Books, a division of
Bantam Doubleday Dell Publishing Group, Inc. Its trademark,
consisting of the words "Bantam Books" and the portrayal of a
rooster, is Registered in U.S. Patent and Trademark Office and in
other countries. Marca Registrada. Bantam Books, 666 Fifth
Avenue, New York, New York 10103

PRINTED IN THE UNITED STATES OF AMERICA

S   0 9 8 7 6 5 4 3 2

**For Mike, Leonard,
and the rest of the Chicago boys**

I figure that Mom and Dad were having some kind of trouble and needed to go away by themselves. Dad was complaining a lot about his job, I remember, and he and Mom were getting into a lot of arguments. Something was on their minds, or they would never have gone away and left me with Leslie. Leslie is my sister. She was seventeen the summer when all this happened, and she was at her all-time craziest, which is saying a lot if you know Leslie.

Leslie had this summer job, answering the telephone in some office, and she was supposed to take care of me, and see that I got fed, and keep me out of trouble while Mom and Dad went to a resort in Colorado. They made a big point of apologizing to me for not taking me along, which was okay with me, since from what I could gather, there was nothing to do where they were going but look at scenery. I have never been able to understand what the big deal is about scenery. I mean, it is very nice if there are some big mountains or something in the background while you are *doing* something, but just standing around all day and saying, "What a lovely view," strikes me as sort of dumb.

They asked Leslie if she was sure she could take care of things, and did she understand everything she was supposed to do, and did she have any questions—about once every five minutes for three days. The rest of the time they ran around packing stuff and writing notes for Leslie. They wrote maybe two thousand notes and taped them up all over the kitchen—recipes and when the laundryman comes and the telephone number of the police, the hospital, the resort in Colorado, all our relatives, all their friends. In fact they wrote down everybody's telephone number in McDonaldsville. They might as well have just taped the telephone directory to the wall. I suppose they felt guilty about going on a vacation without us, but I didn't especially want to go, and Leslie, as I pointed out, is crazy, and there is no way to tell what she wants to do. By the way, I am twelve, was eleven at the time I'm telling about, and perfectly able to take care of myself. Leslie, on the other hand, needs constant watching, but I didn't say anything about that when Mom and Dad were getting ready for their trip.

By the time Mom and Dad left, I was practically praying for them to go. They were starting to make me nervous. Every few minutes one of them would explain how they hated to leave me behind, but they had to get away by themselves. A couple of times Mom decided that she couldn't desert her babies, and there was some crying and hollering. Finally, after going over the whole list of instructions one more time, they took off, leaving me in Leslie's capable hands.

Twenty-four hours later, my big sister had left with her creepy friends on a two-week camping trip to Cape Cod. Typical. At least she didn't do a number before leaving like Mom and Dad. She just came into my room and said, "Victor, I forgot all about it, but I told these kids I'd go to Cape Cod with them. Will you be okay by yourself for a few days?" I told her I'd be fine. She threw some stuff into her canvas bag, split the household money with me, promised to be back before Mom and Dad, made me promise not to tell them she wasn't around, and took off. Her main friend, Gloria Schwartz, and a lot of other hippies came and got her in this real old station wagon full of tents and banjos, and pots and pans. I went outside and told them I'd be surprised if they ever got out of the state in a wreck like that. They all said stuff like "Far out!" and "Heavy!" and all that dumb talk, and drove off in a black cloud of burning oil. I could hear the valves rattle after they were out of sight.

I really thought Leslie would be back by lunchtime after the car broke down, but apparently they made it. About ten o'clock there was a phone call from the place where Leslie worked, asking why she hadn't come in. I told them that she couldn't come to work for a couple of weeks because she was having a baby. It was the best thing I could think of on the spur of the moment. The lady who called didn't say anything for a while, then she said good-bye, and we both hung up.

This particular summer I didn't have much to do. Most of the kids I knew were away at camp, including my best friend, Howard Foster. I had been to camp the year before, and found out I was allergic to everything that grew there. Between being allergic and poison ivy and bee stings and breaking my arm when I fell off the roof of the cabin, there didn't seem to be much point in going back.

All summer I had been going to the McDonaldsville Municipal Pool every day. It only costs fifteen cents to get in if you are a kid, plus ten cents for a locker, and maybe a dime for a grape soda. If you go in the morning, there are only a bunch of little kids who come with their day camps, and the swimming classes that the people at the pool give. That is all happening in the shallow end, so the deep end is almost empty. I'm a good swimmer. I was all ready for my Junior Lifesaving test before I broke my arm at camp. I have my Advanced Swimmer card, though, which means I can swim in the deep end any time. In the afternoon the pool starts to get crowded. Bigger kids come and start horsing around in the deep water. That's when I go home. I am serious about swimming.

On the day Leslie started on her hippie trip to Cape Cod, I didn't go to the pool. I had a few things to do. First I had to keep Mom and Dad from

4

finding out that Leslie was gone. If they knew, they would probably drop everything and come home, which was not called for since I figured I was in much better shape by myself than with Leslie, who was likely to burn down the house or something.

I went to Leslie's room and rummaged around in her desk. I found what I was looking for—some letters she had written to some boyfriend and then came to her senses and didn't mail. The letters made pretty disgusting reading, but each one was signed, "Love, Leslie." I got out her bottle of purple ink and practiced signing her name. Then I typed ten letters on her typewriter. They don't have typing in the sixth grade, so it was hard to get the letters looking right. I made a lot of mistakes and wasted a lot of her little blue note paper. I finally got them all done. They were pretty much alike.

Dear Mom and Dad,
    Hope you are having a good time. Victor is behaving himself. We are getting along o.k. Please don't worry about us, and have a nice vacation.
                    Love,
                        Leslie

Then I found ten envelopes, addressed them, put stamps on them, and stacked them on the table by the front door. All I had to do was mail one every day. Mom and Dad would probably never figure out that Leslie wouldn't remember to write to them. They would be so pleased that they would just

5

decide that she suddenly went sane or something. When they got back and she was as crazy as ever, they would think she had a relapse.

I also made plans in case they called. If they called, it would be early in the evening so that they'd be sure to catch us both awake. I would just say that Leslie was out on a date. This would cheer them up too, because Leslie almost never went out on dates and spent most of her time complaining about it. I could do the same thing if Aunt Mildred called. The icebox was full, and there were about a thousand TV dinners in the freezer, so I didn't have any problem about food. Leslie had left me with plenty of money. Everything was organized.

By the time I had finished writing the letters and figuring everything out, it was pretty late, so I put a TV dinner in the oven—Salisbury steak with creamed corn and mashed potatoes. Then I got ready to watch the Walter Cronkite show. Walter Cronkite is my favorite television star. That's another reason I haven't got many friends at school. Most of the kids like these rock groups like "The Vermin" and "The Scum" and some of these dumb singers who smile all the time and have aluminum foil glued to their jeans. The kids who like those guys think I'm some kind of freak because I'm a Walter Cronkite fan.

Anyway, Walter Cronkite isn't on very much in the summer because that's when he takes his vacation and Roger Mudd fills in for him. I watch the show anyway, because if something really big were to happen, Walter would come straight from his vacation to take over. Another thing I like about when Roger Mudd does the show is the possibility that Walter will die (not that I wish him any harm) on his vacation, and a news flash will come in while Roger Mudd is on the air. Or he wouldn't have to die—he could be trapped underwater in a Volkswagen bus with only enough air for two hours, and Roger Mudd could describe the rescue attempts. Then the Navy divers would get Walter out, and he would say, "That's the way it is," and sort of salute into the camera, and the news program would fade out into the coffee ads. Or it might be good if he did die after all, just after the Navy divers got him out of the sunken bus. Then he could say, "That's the way it is," as his last words. There are a lot of possibilities to the Walter Cronkite show. I used to try to get some of the other kids interested in it, and maybe set up a Walter Cronkite fan club, but they didn't even take it seriously, and I got a reputation as a crazy.

I was eating my TV dinner and watching Roger Mudd. It was very nice. He's no Walter Cronkite, but he always does a good show. Usually people are talking and making noise around the house when I'm watching the news, but this time it was really nice. No Mom, no Dad, no Leslie. Just me and Roger Mudd and my TV dinner. I decided to stay up and watch the late news too. I had never seen the late news. In fact, I had never seen anything on television after ten o'clock, which is my bedtime. I was pretty excited at the idea of watching television as late as I wanted.

I got the magazine with the TV listings from the top of the television. The late news came on at eleven o'clock. In between there was a game show where people got prizes for guessing how much things cost, like a carload of assorted sausages. If they could guess how much the sausages were worth, they could have them, and an icebox, and a car, and a lot of other stuff. There was a movie about a guy who is a doctor who rides around the country on a motorcycle and doesn't tell anyone he's a doctor, and then when they get into accidents, or get sick, or have babies, he takes care of them. Then he gets on his motorcycle. I went and got my model airplane kit to work on while I waited for the late news.

I spread some newspapers in front of the TV set and got to work on my model. It was a DC-10 airliner. Authentic in Every Detail, it said on the box. Probably when Walter Cronkite goes to cover news stories in China and places like that, he flies in airplanes like it. I was thinking about how his plane could be forced down in Tibet, which is near China in the high mountains, and nobody would know what happened to him. Then Roger Mudd would be reporting it on the news, and Walter Cronkite could fix the radio in the plane and call the television station and tell them where the plane had crashed and where to send rescue parties. Roger Mudd could put Walter Cronkite's voice on the air, and he could tell how the plane had crashed in the mountains, and how everybody was getting along, and then he could finish the program for Roger

8

Mudd. "That's the way it is," Walter Cronkite could say.

I got a lot done on the tail section of my model. The movie about the doctor who rides a motorcycle was only fair. It was made someplace where there were mountains right alongside of the ocean, probably California, and there were lots of scenes of the doctor riding on top of cliffs over the water. The story was sort of dumb. He meets this girl who hurt her leg, and she's getting gangrene, but she won't go to a doctor because she doesn't trust anybody, so the doctor on the motorcycle plays his guitar for her, and then she trusts him and he takes her to the hospital. There were some good fried chicken commercials, and I thought about putting another TV dinner in the oven to eat with the late news.

I decided to settle for some chocolate chip cookies and a glass of milk. I was going to clean up the place where I was working on my model, but I remembered that I was all alone in the house, and it wouldn't be in anyone's way. I left it just where it was. I turned down the lights and got ready to watch the late news.

The guy who does the late news has a beard! His name is Bob Barney and he's real good. He giggles, sort of, in the wrong places when he tells news stories, and he's bald, and you can see the lights in the TV studio shining off the top of his head. I was really impressed with him. I think he's almost in Walter Cronkite's class. There's also a little fat guy who does the weather forecast. He's good too. And they do news that doesn't get on the early news show. The show comes from Hogboro, which is just a few miles south of McDonaldsville, and they do stories about things that happen right around here. They even did a story about a guy who got arrested right at the McDonaldsville pool where I go every day! It was a great show.

I wasn't the least bit tired. I felt just fine, sitting in the dark living room with the set on. The only light in the room was the blue light from the television set. I could see my partly finished model airplane on the sheets of newspaper in front of the set, like Walter Cronkite's airliner forced down in the snowfields of Tibet.

I was sort of thinking about the airplane, the news had ended, and I wasn't paying any attention to the ads. A guy dressed up in an apron was in a supermarket telling two ladies how soft this toilet paper was, when a huge gorilla came up behind him and just picked him up and ate him. Like a cookie. Two bites. It all happened so fast that I wasn't sure if I had really seen it. As I said, I wasn't really paying attention.

Then a movie came on. It wasn't stupid like the one about the doctor on a motorcycle. This was a wonderful monster movie about a mad scientist who has an island and does horrible experiments there. This scientist, who is fat and always carries a big whip, takes all kinds of animals and turns them into men. Some of them are more like men, and some of them are more like animals. They all hate the mad scientist, because they would rather have been animals, but they are afraid of him too.

Every night the scientist cracks his whip and makes the man-animals repeat the same thing.

He says, "What is the law?"

They say, "We shall eat no meat. We shall walk on two legs. We shall spill no blood. ARE WE NOT MEN?"

Then they all sort of growl and dance around, and the mad scientist cracks his whip again. At the end all the monsters go crazy and tear the mad scientist to pieces and set the whole island on fire. All in all, it was about the best movie I ever saw. There was a lot of screaming and blood-curdling stuff in it. In fact it was so good that I forgot all about how scary it was and that I was all alone in the middle of the night. Until it was over, that is. Then, during the commercial for a school where you can learn to be a truck driver, I remembered every scary, screaming, blood-curdling thing that happened in the monster movie. I thought about the dreams I was going to have, and all of a sudden I felt a cold chill.

I was almost at the point of running into the kitchen and looking up the number of the resort where Mom and Dad were staying, when the lizard band came onto the screen. These were real lizards, not people dressed up as lizards, and they played regular musical instruments. There were five or six of them. At first it was scarier than the movie, especially the close-ups, but as the lizards

11

played and swayed together, I sort of got used to it. The music was very strange. It wasn't like anything I'd ever heard before. It sounded funny at first, but I got used to it very fast, and then I liked it more than anything I'd ever heard. I didn't think about liking it—I didn't think about anything. I just listened to the music and swayed with the lizards. Every time they stopped playing, I felt afraid that they wouldn't start again—but I don't know when they stopped because I woke up on the couch in the morning. The television was still on, hissing, with no picture—just a bunch of little dots jumping around. There was the model airplane, the plate with a few cookie crumbs, and the glass with a little milk at the bottom.

2

At first, when I woke up, I listened for sounds of people in the house. Then I remembered that everyone was gone. I fixed myself some cornflakes and milk. I sat in the kitchen eating my breakfast. It was very quiet, quieter than it had been the night before. I had always heard people say, "It was so quiet you could hear yourself think," and I always thought it was a silly figure of speech. How can you hear yourself think? Now, in the quiet kitchen, I really could hear myself think.

I washed the dirty dishes from breakfast and the night before, and then I sat around thinking about what I would do that day. I didn't feel like going to the pool. It seemed to me that I ought to do something that took advantage of being on my own. One thing I had been planning to try was smoking. Mom had left a pack of her lemon-flavored cigarettes on the kitchen counter. I lit one up. It felt good sitting at the kitchen table holding the cigarette. If I knew how to make coffee, I could have tried that too, but I had to settle for the lemon-flavored cigarette and a glass of milk. I was afraid the cigarette would make me cough. It didn't though—it just made me sick. I got dizzy and started to sweat, and wound up throwing up my cornflakes and milk. So much for smoking.

I just hung around for a couple of hours, looking at magazines and getting over being sick. I thought about the stuff I had seen on television and wondered what Walter Cronkite was doing on his vacation. I wished I could remember some of the tunes the lizard band was playing. I checked the TV listings for the night before, and there wasn't anything about them. The last listing was the monster movie, *The Island of Dr. Morbo.*

Then I got the idea of going to Hogboro. Kids from McDonaldsville just about never go to the city of Hogboro, even though there is a bus every twenty minutes, and it takes less than half an hour. I myself had only been in Hogboro a few times, when Mom and Dad took us to dinner and a movie, and once there was a school trip to a museum. Another time I had gone with Mom on the bus, and we went to a couple of big department stores. When we got back, she said that the stores weren't any better than the ones in McDonaldsville, and being in the city made her feel insecure. I thought the stores in Hogboro were a lot better than the ones in McDonaldsville. For one thing, they weren't all on one level, and you rode up and down on these moving stairways. And they were crowded. People, all kinds, were everywhere.

In McDonaldsville, you never get to see a crowd. Maybe you will see a whole lot of people at a basketball game, or something like that, but it isn't a crowd. The people all know each other, or if they don't, they should. I mean they're all the same, and they are all there for the same reason, and they all know just what kind of house everybody else lives in and what sort of car they have, because they have a house and a car just like it. A crowd is a whole bunch of different people, all of them doing something a little bit different—they're all alone in the middle of a whole lot of people they don't know. If you were to meet somebody you knew in a real crowd, it would be a big surprise.

The bus stop was four blocks from my house. I picked up one of the forged letters to Mom and Dad to drop in the mailbox and went to wait for the bus.

When the bus came, there was hardly anybody on it. Every morning the buses are full of men going to work in Hogboro, and every night they all ride back. The rest of the day the buses run back and forth, mostly empty, with maybe a few ladies going shopping. I sat by a window and watched as we went through the familiar streets of McDonalds-ville, shopping centers, hamburger stands, houses. Then we got to streets I didn't know. The houses got closer together, and there were fewer trees. The bus passed big factories and apartment buildings. Everything seemed to be made of brick.

I didn't know exactly why I was going to Hogboro. I just sort of thought of doing it, and did it. The bus was rolling down a big wide street, and I felt very good about the whole idea.

The bus had not picked anyone up for quite a while. I figured that we were already in Hogboro, or close to it. We were stopped at a corner, when the bus driver shouted out the window, "Hey! Chicken Man!" The driver opened the door, and a very old black man got on. He didn't pay any fare. All the people on the bus were smiling—they seemed to know who the Chicken Man was. He was wearing an old raincoat and a rumpled old hat. There was a string around his neck, and hanging from it were a toy telephone, a baby doll, little bottles of beer, a couple of bells, and a lot of other junk.

I was wondering why he was called the Chicken Man, when he took his hat off, and there on his head, sitting calmly as though she were on a nest, was a big fat white chicken.

"Hey, Chicken Man!" one of the passengers shouted. "Have your chicken do some tricks!" The Chicken Man did a couple of dance steps in the aisle of the bus. Then he tapped his chicken with his long bony finger, and it hopped off onto his shoulder. The chicken did all sorts of tricks. She danced on the old man's shoulders and clucked into the toy telephone, drank beer from a little bottle, and at the end of the act, hopped onto the old man's head and settled down so he could put his hat over her.

At the end of the chicken act everybody clapped and cheered. Nobody offered the Chicken Man any money, and he didn't pass his hat or anything. I guessed he didn't do that for a living, just to entertain people.

When the Chicken Man had finished his act I noticed we were already inside the Hogboro bus terminal.

3

The bus terminal was noisy and dirty and crowded. People were carrying suitcases and bundles and babies. A bunch of soldiers were standing together, talking loud and laughing. They had shiny boots. Everybody seemed to be in a big rush, or else bored, waiting for a bus that was hours away.

I went out into the street. Car horns were tooting and buses were rumbling, and everyone was moving fast. I stood still for a while and watched. The people were passing by like a long freight train, and I felt like a car stopped at a crossing. I couldn't move. I couldn't really see the street, just the people passing.

Then I was moving too. All of a sudden I was in the stream of people, going fast. It felt as though I were being partly carried. It wasn't like regular walking. It was almost like swimming in a race. I was going pretty fast, and getting hot and sweaty.

Store windows and movie canopies with thousands of little light bulbs flashed past. Sometimes it was a blur, and sometimes things stood out clearly, as I sped past with the crowd—Chop Suey, Pants Pressed, 3 Big Features, Discounts. The signs were red and green and blue, made of light bulbs and neon tubing.

After a while the crowd started to thin out and slow down. There weren't as many lighted signs, and the buildings were darker and older looking.

I kept walking. There were little private houses between the office buildings, with little gardens in front, mostly weeds. The stores were smaller than the ones near the bus terminal. They didn't have electric signs. A lot of them were empty. The whole neighborhood was sort of run down. Paint was peeling off the front doors, and there were a lot of cracks in the sidewalk. Grass grew out of the cracks. There weren't many people walking, and there weren't many cars. People were leaning out of windows, watching the street with their elbows on pillows. Every window was open—not an air conditioner in sight. The whole place smelled of old bricks.

I had never seen anything like it before. McDonaldsville is all new houses, or neat streets of old houses with fresh paint, and shopping centers with big parking lots. Nobody keeps his window open in the summertime.

I stopped in front of an empty store. There were big glass windows on both sides of the door, which was padlocked. It was dark and dusty inside. I could see right through the store and out the back windows, which opened onto a sort of yard with leafy weeds and trees of paradise swaying in the breeze. It looked like two television screens showing a color picture of a green jungle. I looked at the two bright squares of green in the dark store for a long time—then I noticed something else.

Taped to the window, on the inside, was an old record album cover. It had been in color once, but the sun had faded it until it was all different shades of brownish yellow. It was so faded, you really had to stare at it to make it out. There was a picture of five lizards, and over them was printed, The Modern Lizard Quintet Plays Mozart. It was very faded. It took a long time to figure out what it said, and what the picture showed.

The lizard band had made a record! I decided to look for it. As I said, I'm not all that interested in the records the other kids listen to, but I thought I'd like to have a record of the lizards. I could play it on Leslie's portable stereo. I was sure there would be a record store near the bus terminal. I turned around and started walking back. It was starting to drizzle. The drops made dark spots on the sidewalk, and the brick smell was getting stronger.

I was walking fast. I wanted to get to the record store before the rain got heavy. I didn't make it. There was a flash and a crash, and I ducked into a doorway just before it hit. It was as though a big bucket had been turned over. What a rain! It made a noise like rattling marbles in a can. I thought the rain was making a clucking noise like a chicken, too, until I looked around and saw that I was sharing the doorway with the Chicken Man.

4

"**C**laudia doesn't like this rain very much," the Chicken Man said.

"Is Claudia the name of your chicken?" I asked.

"It isn't the name of my lizard," the Chicken Man laughed, a high weird laugh. It scared me. I was scared the minute I saw him. I'm not used to black people. There are only five black kids in our school, and you never get a chance to talk to them, because there is always a crowd of kids around them showing how they're not prejudiced. I had made up my mind to get a chance to talk to this one kid, Melvyn. He's the smallest black kid, and he wears glasses. I figured I'd start with him and see how it went. The Chicken Man was not only black, but old and scary, and he had that weird laugh, and his skin fitted him like an old raincoat.

"Did you say lizard?" I asked.

"No, did you?" Then the Chicken Man laughed again. I wished he wouldn't do that.

"I saw you on the bus today." I wished it would stop raining hard so I could get out of there.

"Claudia sure doesn't like this rain," the Chicken Man said. "It makes her bones hurt—arthritis, I suppose—she's a very old chicken." Claudia was making angry, muffled, clucking noises under the old man's hat.

"Is that what you do?"

"What?"

"Just go around with the chicken—"

"Claudia."

"—with Claudia, and do tricks and stuff?"

"I saw you on the bus too," the Chicken Man said. "Did you find what you were looking for?"

"Well, I wasn't exactly looking for anything."

"Yes, but did you find it?"

"Find what?"

"Maybe you're looking for something, and don't know what it is," the Chicken Man said. "Maybe you don't even know that you're looking. You sure looked to me like you were looking for something."

"When? Just now?"

"Just now, just before, on the bus—all the time. You look like you're on the track of something or other.

"Well, just now I was thinking about looking for a record. I was just going to look for a record store when the rain started." Claudia was making a sort of moaning noise.

"I sure wish this rain would stop. Claudia is getting uncomfortable." The Chicken Man was

23

stroking his hat, trying to calm down his chicken. "What's your name?"

"Victor."

"Look here, Victor." The Chicken Man held out his hand. It was like the branch of a tree; the fingers were dry and wrinkled and bony. I looked into his palm. It was like a really old baseball glove.

"What am I supposed to be looking for?"

"Just look—see what you're looking for." I looked into the Chicken Man's empty palm. Claudia was clucking to herself, the rain was thumping—all of a sudden there was a little green lizard thrashing around in the Chicken Man's palm. That did it! I was four blocks away when I drew my next breath. I ran through the rain all the way to the bus terminal. A McDonaldsville bus was just pulling out, and I jumped on at the last second. I fell into a seat. I was soaking wet. I was shaking too. That lizard had surprised me. It didn't scare me— I'm not afraid of snakes and spiders and things like that. It wasn't even seeing it appear like that. I knew the Chicken Man could do tricks. The thing I kept wondering about all through the bus ride home was how the Chicken Man knew about the lizards. Did he really know, or was it just a coincidence? My shirt was sticking to the bus seat, and my back was sticking to my shirt. There was a fairly large puddle forming under my seat. I was still dripping when the bus stopped near my house. I stepped off into a puddle about four feet deep and sloshed home.

I decided I'd better come in through the kitchen door so I wouldn't soak the carpet. Just as I came around to the back of the house, there was a clap of thunder, and another cloudburst—just to make sure I was *really* wet. I just stood in the kitchen, dripping. I decided I'd undress in the kitchen, wring out my clothes over the sink, and then throw them down into the basement where the dryer is. First I took all the stuff out of my pockets and piled it on the kitchen table. I got my clothes off, threw them down the basement stairs, and went to get a towel and some dry clothes. Once I was dry, I looked at the clock—news time soon. I put a TV fried-chicken dinner in the oven. I started putting the stuff from the kitchen table back into my pockets. Everything was there—house keys, wallet, knife, police whistle, comb in handmade leather case (from camp the summer before), some ballpoint pens, a little notebook, a magnifying glass, a pipe (I don't smoke it. It's a cracked one of my father's, just like Walter Cronkite's pipe).

There was also a card. I didn't remember seeing it before. It was printed in blue letters on pink paper, and it was soggy. I picked it up.

HERR DOKTOR PROFESSOR HORACE
KUPECKIE, Plt.D.
(The Chicken Man)

Representing Claudia, the dancing Chicken, Dreams Explained, Lost Articles located, Psychiatry, Telepathy, Saws Sharpened.

By Appointment—City Bus Terminal—
Hgbro.

25

25

The Chicken Man must have slipped the card into my pocket. He was a pretty good magician, there wasn't any doubt about that. Back in my house, the whole thing didn't seem so scary. The Chicken Man didn't seem mean, just weird and spooky. I got the TV warmed up. There was a game show where the contestants jump into a deep pit with greased sides. They have to wear a special suit with no pockets. At the bottom of the pit there's a million dollars in small bills. They have half a minute to stuff as much money as they can into their mouth, and scramble up the greased sides of the pit. The audience screams a lot. Nobody ever winds up with much more than a hundred dollars.

The oven timer went off just as the news program started. I got my fried chicken and watched the news. I wasn't really able to pay attention. I kept thinking about Herr Doktor Professor Horace Kupeckie, Plt.D., and the trick he had done with the lizard. It was sort of bothering me. I guessed a good magician could make something appear like that—but a lizard! How did he know I was thinking about lizards? The doorway where I met the Chicken Man was not far from the empty store window where I was looking at the lizard album cover. Maybe he saw me looking at that, and guessed that I'd be thinking about a lizard. I had seen a magician at a school show who would tell you to pick a card and then think about it, and then he would show you the card. It was kind of odd that Doktor Professor Kupeckie had a lizard in his pocket. On the other hand, he kept a chicken under his hat. Maybe he had a whole lot of animals stashed in his raincoat. I felt a little embarrassed about running away like that. Probably I had hurt Professor Kupeckie's feelings. He may have just been trying to be friendly and show me a trick.

Roger Mudd was telling how the President likes to eat cottage cheese with catsup on it for lunch—the telephone rang. It was Mom calling to see how things were going. I told her that everything was fine. She wanted to talk to Leslie, but I told her she went bowling with Gloria Schwartz. Then she wanted to know if I had eaten my supper. I told her I was eating it right now. Then she wanted to know what I was having, and I told her. Then Dad got on and asked me all the same questions. Then Mom got on again, and she asked me all the same questions again. Then Dad got on and gave me a bunch of advice, mostly the same stuff they had told me before they left. Then Mom got on, and she said everything that Dad had said. I was trying to stretch the telephone cord so I could see Roger Mudd. It was hard to see the screen, but I thought I saw a little lizard head peeking over Roger's shoulder—just for a second. Mom and Dad finally hung up, and I ran back to the TV, but there wasn't any lizard. I wasn't sure if I had seen it or not. I decided I was for sure going to wait up for the lizard band.

I had a look at the TV listings. There was nothing about the lizards. The late movie was *Invasion of the Pod People*. It sounded good. I wondered why Roger Mudd would have a lizard on his shoulder. Some people keep lizards as pets, but Roger Mudd wouldn't bring his lizard on television. I mean, maybe he would, but Walter would never do such a thing, and he wouldn't let Roger do it either. I probably imagined it (not that I go in for imagining things—I'm not that sort of kid). Still, I was pretty shook up earlier when Professor Kupeckie did that trick, and I was sort of starting to get lizards on the brain.

Right after the news there was one of these animal programs. There have been a lot of animal programs lately. They are all about alike. They show some kind of wild animal and tell about how in a few years they will all be killed off, and it's a shame and all the fault of human beings. Most of the programs are sponsored by companies that make dog food and stuff like that. I heard Walter Cronkite say that they use whale meat in dog food. I always wonder if the sponsors of the animal programs use whale meat in their dog food. I like the animal programs pretty well; it seems that everybody likes animals, now that they've killed most of them. This time the program was about lizards. I might have known. It was getting to be national lizard week, or something. All of a sudden, I was running into lizards every five minutes. "I'll bet a lizard could get elected president," I thought.

The program was very interesting. There are a lot of different kinds of lizards—all sizes and colors. They didn't seem to have much in the way of personality, but some of them were very pretty. Sometimes I wish we had a color set. The program showed lizards eating bugs, and frogs, and other lizards. It showed them running around, and fighting, and shedding their skins. It didn't show any of them playing the saxophone.

After the animal program there was a police program, with lots of head-bashing, and shooting, and crashing cars, and men hitting women, and dope addicts going crazy, and all that stuff. Those shows are always the same. I worked on my model airplane and sort of half-watched it. Even the commercials were dull. Some big company, maybe an insurance company or an oil company—they didn't even say what they made—they just talked about what a great country America is and showed all these pictures of dumb-looking families smiling at the camera. The other channels all had police shows too, so I was stuck. For part of the time I dozed off on the floor, with my chin resting on the newspaper I had spread out under my model. As a result of falling asleep, part of the wing got glued on crooked. I was holding it while the glue dried, when I dozed off. I had a lot of trouble getting it straightened out, and it still didn't look too neat by the time the late news came on. I hate sloppy work on model airplanes—it sort of ruins them. I'm usually very careful not to have any splops of glue, or lumpy paint, or anything like that. It really frustrated me that my DC-10 had glue bumps on the wing. I hoped the paint would cover them.

I did the cookie and milk thing again, and settled down to watch the late news and the late movie. I turned off most of the lights and got ready to watch Bob Barney. Bob Barney really took my mind off my troubles; he did a first-rate news show again. Really, that guy has a fantastic future ahead of him. One of the things he did that I had never seen before was the man-in-the-street interview. This is how it works. Bob Barney goes out with a tape recorder and a videotape camera. He has a cameraman to work the equipment—Bob Barney just holds the microphone. There's a question; this particular night it was "Should public employees have the right to strike?" Then Bob Barney waits around on a busy street and stops people and asks the question. The first guy was dressed in a suit, and he had horn-rimmed glasses and a little hat. Bob Barney asked him his name.

"My name is Lawrence Lawrence," the man said.

Then Bob Barney asked him the question of the day, "Should public employees have the right to strike?"

"Golly, I never really thought about it," Lawrence Lawrence said.

"Well, you must have some feeling on the question," Bob Barney said. "What's your basic reaction?"

"Well, I'd say, whatever turns them on," Lawrence Lawrence said.

Then Bob Barney stopped a little fat woman with no teeth. Every time she said a swear word, they beeped it out, but you could see her lips moving. "You're *beep* right! My *beep* son's first wife's cousin's boy is a fireman. The way that poor *beep* has to work—it's a *beep* shame. Let the *beep* city *beep beep beep.*"

In the background, coming up the street, was someone in a rumpled raincoat. He wasn't coming straight up the street. He was doing a little turn now and then and sort of shifting from one side of the pavement to the other, snapping his fingers and sort of dipping at the knees. As he got closer, I could see it was the Chicken Man—he was dancing! He was dancing along the sidewalk. Just as the beep lady got through with the question, the Chicken Man was almost filling the picture behind her, dipping and turning and snapping. Next he was on camera, and Bob Barney was asking him his name.

"Lucas Cranach, Jr.," the Chicken Man said.

"Should public employees have the right to strike?" asked Bob Barney.

The Chicken Man was still dipping and snapping his fingers. "Public employees must, of necessity, be divided into two general groups," the Chicken Man said, "those whose function is vital to the health and welfare of the community, and those whose function is mainly clerical, or administrative. Functionaries, such as police, fire department personnel, sanitation workers, and public health workers, have a responsibility which extends beyond the limits of an ordinary job. Although all Americans have the right to collective bargaining, this constitutes a gray area, which has been the subject of much debate. It is to be hoped that, at least in our city, matters of budget and arbitration will be conducted in such a way that the question remains academic."

"Thank you very much, sir," Bob Barney said.

"Dig it," said the Chicken Man. "Can I say hello to my friend Victor?"

"I'm sorry," Bob Barney said, "Federal Communications Commission rules prohibit using the media for personal messages."

"Dig it—forget about it, Victor," the Chicken Man said, and the Chicken Man, also known as Herr Doktor Professor Horace Kupeckie, Plt.D., also known as Lucas Cranach, Jr., dipped and spun and snapped off camera.

This last weird thing knocked me out completely. I didn't know what to think. Except that every kid in my school has taken a battery of psychological tests—and I came out 100 percent normal and average in every one—I would have thought that maybe I was going crazy. I never heard of so many coincidences! Lizards! And the Chicken Man turning up everywhere! And saying hello to me on television! It was too much!

The late movie snapped me out of it. I was mainly worrying about all the crazy things that had happened to me all day, but the picture caught my interest, and soon I was paying pretty close attention to it. It was almost as good as the one I had seen the night before.

In this movie, *Invasion of the Pod People*, little seeds from outer space float down into everybody's basement. Then the seeds start growing into giant pods—like watermelons, only much bigger. Nobody ever finds one. After the pods get to be full grown, they break open, and out steps an exact replica of each person who lives in the house. The replicas sneak upstairs and eat the people. Then they take their places. They are exactly like the other people—the real earth people—in every way, except the pod people have no emotions and have terrible taste. The earth people have no idea that they are being replaced.

Then this one earth person finds out what is happening. He goes around spotting pod people. The pod people smile all the time and put catsup on everything. He tries to save himself and his girl friend. It turns out that they are the only two people in town who have not been replaced. Their replacements are waiting to eat them, but they can only do it if the earth person is asleep. Finally they get the girl friend, but the one guy escapes. He's going to warn the rest of the world, but he doesn't know if the rest of the world has gone pod or not. It just ends there—with the guy on the highway trying to hitch a ride, and all that passes him are trucks full of big pods. A great movie—much better than your usual science fiction, because the outer-space creatures win, or at least have a chance. And the movie leaves it up to you.

I was pretty tired after all I had been through during the day, and I actually had to hold my eyes open for the last part of the movie. I was determined to wait up for the lizards to come on. They did, but I must have fallen asleep almost at once, because when I woke up—on the couch again—I hardly remembered anything about the lizard show. I barely remembered that they had been on; it seemed like a dream. In fact, everything that had happened the day before seemed sort of like a dream. I felt woozy and tired out, the way you feel when you've had a whole bunch of bad dreams. I almost had decided that it was a dream, when I saw the Chicken Man's card on the kitchen table, with the corners curling up.

It was real—at least most of it. I didn't feel too well. I thought about the bumpy glue on the model airplane wing. My whole life was getting bumpy like that, and I was feeling dissatisfied. I like things neat. This situation wasn't neat at all. I decided that I was going to do something about it. Up till now, things had just been happening—not even happening *to* me—just happening in front of me. I wanted to make some things happen.

First I made some frozen orange juice and toasted a frozen blueberry muffin. While the muffin was in the toaster, I got a pencil and paper. I ate my muffin and wrote:

1. Lizards on television, playing music.
2. Lizard album cover in store window.
3. Lizard in Chicken Man's hand.
4. Lizard on Roger Mudd's shoulder.
5. Animal program about lizards.
6. The Chicken Man saying hello on television.

I studied my list. Except for the animal program about lizards, which was only weird because of the other things, all the items on my list were not normal things to happen in my life. They had all happened in two days. They all had to do with lizards, and/or the Chicken Man.

Now, what was I going to do about it? What would Walter Cronkite or Mr. Hatch, the Science teacher do about it? I thought that, probably, they would double check all the information. I started double checking. I got the TV section and checked the listings for the whole week. Nothing that sounded like the lizard band was listed anywhere. There was nothing at all listed at the time period when I had seen the lizard band. The animal program was listed, and it was about lizards. That was okay. Then I called Information in Hogboro and got the number of the TV station, WLIZ—it's funny that I never noticed those call letters before. I wondered if I should add them to my list. I decided not to, because it had those letters before this whole business got started. I dialed the TV station. A lady answered.

"I'd like to ask some questions about the programs on your station last night," I said.

"Please hold on," the lady said.

Then a man's voice said, "May I help you?"

"Did you have a program with lizards late last night?"

" 'Animals of the World' featured lizards—it was broadcast at seven-thirty."

"Was there another program, a music program, with lizards late at night—after the late movie?"

"Our last program was the late movie, *Invasion of the Pod People*. After that here were some public service messages, a moment of inspiration, and we went off the air."

"Off the air?"

"Yes, turned off the lights, locked the doors, went home—off the air."

"One other question. Does Roger Mudd ever have a lizard on his shoulder when he does the news?"

Click—buzz, the man had hung up on me. I can't say I blamed him. He probably thought I was a nut. Anyway, I had found out that the TV station wasn't broadcasting the lizard band—but I had seen them. There were several possibilities. One, I was crazy, or I had imagined the lizards. But, as I said, I don't go in for imagining things, and it hadn't been six months since I took all those psychological tests. Besides, I didn't feel crazy. Two, the lizards were getting into the TV station after it closed, turning everything on, and putting out their own program. That sounded a little farfetched, but lizards who can play clarinets and saxophones might be capable of anything. Three, the lizard program was coming from someplace other that the TV station, and our TV set was picking up their show. I couldn't think of any more possibilities. I went over the three again. One, was I crazy? I went into the bathroom and looked in the mirror. I looked as sane as anybody in the world; I was sure I wasn't crazy. That left possibilities two and three. Either the lizards were broadcasting from the TV station, or they were broadcasting from some other TV station. I would have to get more information before I decided.

Next was the Chicken Man. Was he connected to all the lizard stuff, or was that just a coincidence? I looked at his card. "By Appointment—City Bus Terminal—Hgbro," it said. I didn't know how to make an appointment with him. Maybe I could just run into him at the bus terminal and make an appointment then. I'd have to go into Hogboro again. That would also give me a chance to double check the album cover in the store window. I felt good about all the progress I was making. I got ready to go to Hogboro.

I didn't forget to mail another phony letter to Mom and Dad. I was glad that Leslie wasn't around, what with the lizard and Chicken Man mystery going on. She would probably have gotten hysterical. She doesn't like lizards and snakes and things like that. Probably, she would have started screaming for her mommy, and calling the police, and generally making it impossible to get to the bottom of things. I had an investigation on my hands, and I certainly didn't need my crazy sister to make it harder. You can be sure that Walter Cronkite doesn't have to put up with things like that.

On the bus, I thought about what I would do in the city. I was going to look for the Chicken Man, examine the record album cover, and in general keep a sharp eye out for lizards of all kinds. I had my magnifying glass and my notebook. I was going to get the facts. I felt like Walter Cronkite working on a big news story. I got out my notebook and made a couple of notes. "Lizard," I wrote, and "Chicken."

I was the first one off the bus when it stopped in the terminal. I had a lot to do, and it was already ten in the morning. I looked around for the Chicken Man. I didn't see him. I set off for the empty store with the lizard album cover.

The crowds of people in the street didn't bother me as much as they had the day before. I wasn't so much carried along by the moving crowd, as moving through it. I found I could shift around slow-moving people and never break my pace. I had more time to look around, and I wasn't as nervous. I had a chance to look at the people. They all looked straight ahead. It seemed to me that a person walking toward me was going to crash right into me. Then, at the last minute, we'd just miss each other. It was like a game. All the men had suits and hats on, and the women clicked along on little high-heeled shoes. Everybody had this real serious expression, like they were very important and busy. They all had a tendency to walk in a straight line, and in my rubber-soled sneakers, I could weave in and out and around and pass everybody. It was fun. I felt like a little sports car moving through a lot of trucks.

When I got into the older neighborhood where there weren't so many pedestrians, I slowed down. It was pretty much the same as the day before, except the sun was shining, and I saw something I had never seen before—a horse and wagon! It was this real old wagon with tires off an old truck or something—wooden spokes—and it was piled up with broken chairs and old bedsprings and bundles of old clothes. There was an old guy driving it, and the horse looked old too. He was gray and sort of scuffed-looking and he had a hat! The horse had a hat, with holes cut out for his ears! I didn't know that anybody used a horse and wagon anymore.

When I got to the empty store the album cover was gone! There were some marks on the inside of the window where the Scotch tape had been, but no album cover! The door still had the padlock on it. The trees and weeds were still waving outside the back windows. The same dead flies were still lying on the windowsill, but the album cover was gone.

I heard a rumbling sound behind me and turned to see a giant green lizard—about nine feet long! His mouth was open, and he had rows of little sharp-looking teeth, and a red tongue. "This is it," I thought. "Either I'm going to die or go nuts." The lizard was moving down the street a little above eye level. He was roaring—making a noise like a bus. Above his head was printing, and underneath him. He was printed too! Explore the Wonders of the Natural World, it said above the printed lizard. Visit the Hogboro Zoo, it said underneath him. Take the Special Zoo Bus, it said under that. It was an advertising poster. I only thought the lizard was real for maybe a quarter of a second. I was already telling myself that I knew it all along. But my mouth was very dry. The bus with the lizard poster moved away.

7

I got out my notebook:

7. Realistic Lizard Poster. (Take special zoo bus.)

My mouth felt really dry. I decided it wasn't just the surprise of the giant lizard on the bus. It was also the surprise of seeing that someone had removed the album cover. Someone was trying to hide clues. I wondered if it could be the Chicken Man. He had seen me looking at the album cover. Maybe there were a whole lot of people who didn't want me to find out about the lizards. Maybe the guy at the TV station was lying to me over the telephone. I decided that I'd better get a grape soda.

There was a little store on the corner. It sold magazines and cigars and candy, and it had a soda fountain. I went in. It was dark and it smelled sort of sweet and damp. They had all kinds of weird candy in jars. In each jar there was a piece of torn-off cardboard and penciled on it was 1¢ or 2¢. There were cards with combs and key chains and corncob pipes and dice and work gloves and little American flags, and all sorts of other stuff hanging behind the counter with the 1¢ and 2¢ candy. A little farther down was this counter made out of black and white stone—marble, I guess. It had stools, and most of them, and most of the counter, had stacks of newspapers piled up. I sat down on the one stool without a stack of newspapers on it. There was a little fat guy moving around behind the counter. He was about as wide as he was tall.

"Don't just sit—say!" he said.

"I beg your pardon?" I said.

"Say! Say! What do you want? How may I serve you, Your Highness?" The little fat guy made a low bow, and disappeared under the chrome faucets behind the soda fountain. He didn't come up again. I sat there waiting for him to straighten up. "Thay! Thay!" he groaned. I could hear him sort of grunting and moaning from somewhere underneath the counter. "Thaaay!"

"I'd like a grape soda, please," I said.

The little fat guy popped up like a cork, "Yes sir. At your service! One grape soda for His Majesty! Coming up!" The little fat guy ran to the end of the counter and shouted into a door that was there at the back of the store, almost hidden by stacks of cartons. "A grape soda for the young tsarevich!" he shouted through the door. Then he ran to the front of the store and shouted out into the street, "A grape soda for a prince of royal blood!" Then he

43

reached under the counter and came up with a thing like a little tiny accordion. "Taa ta ta too!" he shouted and squeezed the little accordion thing, which sounded sour. Then the little fat guy dropped the little accordion and ran to the back of the store where there was a soda cooler. He fished out a bottle of grape soda, draped a little towel over his arm, and ran back to where I was sitting. He showed me the label. Professor Pedwie's Natural Grape Beverage, it said.

"Nineteen seventy-five, an excellent year," the little fat guy said. "Does the young gentleman approve?"

"Sure," I said.

"Sure! Sure!" The little fat guy danced around. "He approves! Order the Cadillac limousine and the estate in France! He approves!" He opened the bottle and handed it to me. "Does the Prince want a straw?"

I had an idea—sort of a hunch. "Excuse me," I said, "Do you know someone called the Chicken Man?"

"Of course, Majesty," the little fat guy said. "He is my friend. He comes here every night. We watch the lizards together."

I almost choked on my grape soda, "You watch the lizards?" I asked.

"Isn't that what I said?" the little fat guy shouted. "You're maybe a music critic? You have something against lizards? You prefer rock and roll? Who asked you? That'll be ten cents for the soda."

44

"No. I mean, I—I watch the lizards too. I'm just surprised—I mean, I'm a friend of the Chicken Man—I mean, I met him—I was sort of looking for him." I dug out a dime and put it on the counter.

"Ah, that's different. Any friend of the Chicken Man is a friend of mine. Would you care to leave a message for him?"

"Just tell him that Victor was looking for him."

"Exactly so. Victor. And my name is Shane Fergussen," the little fat guy said.

"Pleased to meet you," I said.

"Precisely. My good friend, Matthias Grunewald, also known as the Chicken Man, will be here late tonight. Here is the number, if you should care to call him." Shane Fergussen handed me a card. It said:

HUBERT VAN EYCK
(The Chicken Man)
Old and Rare Poultry Books
Investment Counsellor
Bail Bondsman
Telephone   HO7-8937

"You said his name was Matthias Grunewald," I said.

"Without question. His professional name, however, is—" Shane Fergussen took the card back and looked at it—"Hubert Van Eyck." He handed me the card again. I put it in my notebook, and noticed the last note I had made, "Take special zoo bus."

45

"Do you know where I can catch the special zoo bus?" I asked Shane Fergussen.

"Right on the corner. You can't miss it. It's got a big lizard on the side."

I said good-bye to Shane Fergussen and went outside to wait for the bus.

I didn't have long to wait—but not for the bus. A green taxi pulled up. The driver had an enormous cap, like the caps they always show golfers wearing—plaid with a little pom-pom on top and a bill. The cap was so large it completely covered his face.

"Your transport has arrived, man," the cab driver said.

"I beg your pardon?" I asked.

"Wheels! Locomotion! Speed! Make the scene in the green machine!" the cabbie said.

"I'm waiting for the special zoo bus," I said.

"The zoo! Scooby Doo! How true! Enter the vehicle. The zoo! One dollar without the tip, man." The cabbie was pounding on the dashboard with his fists.

"No thanks," I said, "I'll wait for the bus. It only costs a quarter."

"Egad, a proletarian!" the cabbie said. "Let me advise you, Daddy. Don't travel with *hoi polloi,* the many, the common crowd, you dig it? Not when you're on the trail of pleasure and high adventure. Ensconce yourself in this limo and ride in style—fifty cents." The taxicab had a very bad sounding engine. It made a lot of smoke. The whole car was painted green with little yellow squares—like scales.

"All right! Twenty-five cents to the zoo, but I don't play the radio," the cab driver said. There was something familiar about the cab driver's voice. All I could see of him was the gigantic golfer's cap and his brown knuckles on the steering wheel. I got in. There was a card on the back of the driver's seat.

HOGBORO CITY TAXI LICENSE
Charles Swan 04011

On the card was a picture of Charles Swan, the cab driver. He was wearing the golf cap, which cast a shadow over his whole face. All I could see were two eyes peering out of the darkness.

"Goin' to the zoo-oo, sorry but I can't take you; Goin' to the zoo-oo, sorr-i-ee but I can't take you—" Charles Swan was singing. As I said, I am not used to black people. I had an idea that Charles Swan was kidding me. On the other hand, maybe he really talked like that. He was singing another song now, something about Nagasaki.

"It certainly is a nice day for the zoo, Mr. Swan," I said.

48

"Hyuk, hyuk, hyuk, sho' nuff, bless yo' heart, chile, hyuk, hyuk, hyuk!" Charles Swan said. I settled back in my seat. "Hot ginger an' dynamite," Charles Swan sang. I had a funny feeling about Charles Swan. There was something I wanted to ask him, but he always went into the "Hyuk, hyuk, hyuk" thing every time I was sort of clearing my throat, getting ready to try and start a conversation.

The cab was very noisy. There wasn't much in the way of a muffler, and the doors and windows all rattled. Every time we went over a bump, stuff rattled and crashed in the trunk. Charles Swan was singing, and sort of talking to himself the whole time. I wanted to know if he knew the Chicken Man, but he never gave me a chance to talk. The taxi screeched to a stop outside the Hogboro Zoo. Charles Swan stamped on the brakes, and the door swung open all by itself. I handed him his quarter. The engine had died, and he was trying to get the cab started. I started to walk away, then turned back and asked through the window, "Mr. Swan, do you know anything about a guy called the Chicken Man?"

"The Chicken Man?" The engine came to life. There was a rattle and a roar. "Never heard of him." The cab pulled away and left me standing in the gutter. "Bye, Victor!" Charles Swan shouted. I was certain I heard a chicken clucking over the engine noise. I took out my notebook:

8. Chicken Man disguised as cab driver.

I went into the zoo. It occurred to me that I had never been in a zoo before. It had a weird smell. There was a big gate to go through. Then there were a lot of big brick buildings. People were walking around. Most of them had little kids with them. Some of the brick buildings had iron cages along one side. In one of them was a tiger! I went closer and looked at the tiger. It was fantastic! In the next cage was another tiger, and a leopard next to that, and lions! They were beautiful. I spent a long time looking at the big cats. I kept going back to the tigers. I just couldn't believe how beautiful they were. I didn't like the idea of all those animals being kept in cages, but I was glad they were there to look at just the same. I spent the whole day at the zoo, and I never did find out where they keep the lizards, which I had come to look at in the first place.

From the cats, I went to the elephants and the bears. I spent a long time with them. I was just getting to appreciate the different kinds of antelopes, and zebras and buffaloes, when a guard kicked me out of the place—closing time. I had already decided that I was coming back the next day. As a matter of fact, I was planning to come back every day for the rest of my life. I never dreamed that zoos were so wonderful. I mean, I thought they'd be interesting—sort of like the animal programs on television—but looking at the animals for real and hearing them and smelling them—and sometimes the animals look back at you. Wow. It's just great. There was one thing called a lesser kudu that I was looking at just before the guard kicked me out. It had wavy horns and a gray body with thin white stripes and these nice warm eyes. I could still see the lesser kudu on the bus ride to the Hogboro terminal and then home.

I didn't get home until the middle of the news. I switched on Roger Mudd and turned the volume way up so I could hear him in the kitchen. I had forgotten to eat all day. There was stuff to eat for sale in the zoo, and I had bought some peanuts for the bears, but I hadn't remembered to eat anything. I checked the TV dinners. Somehow none of them appealed to me. I thought maybe I'd try some eggs. I had never actually cooked eggs, but I had seen it done often enough.

First I got the frying pan and put about half a stick of butter in it. I turned up the burner under it all the way to get the butter melting, and then I put a couple of slices of whole wheat bread in the toaster. It felt funny to be making a breakfast in the evening. I decided to have some orange juice too. There wasn't any made up, but there were little frozen cans of concentrated orange juice in the freezer. I make this stuff all the time. It's tricky to get the half-frozen lump of orange juice out of the can, and then you have to stir it a lot to get the lump to melt. I was in the middle of this when I noticed that the butter was starting to smoke and sputter. I figured it was ready and got a couple of eggs.

Breaking eggs is much more complicated than it looks. The first one that I tapped on the edge of the pan ran mostly down the outside and sort of got in amongst the burner. I got the next two eggs to go inside the pan, but a lot of shell went in too. I tried picking it out, but it was pretty hot and splattery in the pan, so I left the shell in, figuring I'd pick the pieces out later. At the last minute, I thought I'd like ham and eggs—there was some sliced ham in the icebox—and I threw that in too.

Everything came out at the same time. The eggs were kind of black. So was the ham. So was the toast. The orange juice was just perfect. Everything tasted okay, and I learned something—you can eat egg shells.

Roger Mudd was telling about how the natives of some island in the Pacific were saving their money to buy the President of the United States to be their chief. They wouldn't pay taxes or anything. They had over sixteen thousand dollars saved up. I wondered how they made their money. Fishing, maybe.

After the news, I didn't pay any attention to what was on TV. I had a lot of work to do on my investigation. I had gotten sort of sidetracked at the zoo. I wanted to go over what had been happening during the day. I was certain that Charles Swan was the Chicken Man in disguise. I knew that he went to Shane Fergussen's candy store every night and watched the lizards with him. I had the phone number, HO7-8937. I was sure that the Chicken Man was the key to the lizards. I felt very excited. I was going to find out what was going on. I didn't know how, but I just had this strong feeling that the whole thing was going to make sense soon. I looked at my notebook. None of the things in it made any sense—but they would. I just had to wait for the next thing to happen.

Then it happened! It had been happening all along right in front of me—on TV! I was looking at it. There was this talk show. Ordinarily I never watch talk shows, but as I said, I hadn't bothered to change the channel after the Roger Mudd show. There was this talk show—there was a host with real wavy hair and there were all these guests sitting in a row. One was an actress, and she smiled all the time. She had real big boobs, and the host kept staring at them and making faces and making jokes about how she had real big boobs. The audience screamed every time he made a face, and this actress would smile and sort of move her boobs around. Then there was this other guy—he had a sort of Jungle Jim suit with a fancy scarf, and he was smiling all the time too. Every now and then he'd say something, and the host and the actress would smile and shake their heads, and the actress would move her boobs. And there was a little short guy who was sweating; he'd jump up and down and run around the stage, and the audience would scream. Another woman came out. She was the daughter of somebody famous—I didn't catch the name—and she came out to talk about this cookbook she'd written. She brought out all these weird dishes from her cookbook, like baked beans with marshmallows on them, and sauerkraut with coconut on top. The host tasted the dishes and made faces and rolled his eyes, and the audience screamed. All this stuff was flashing past me a mile a minute. It was happening like a speeded-up movie—and it was very important! I wasn't sure why it was, at first. It seemed like the usual dumb stuff they have on television. There was something special about it, something that had been there all along, only I hadn't ever noticed it. The daughter of the famous somebody was holding up the cookbook. Everybody was clapping. I was noticing something weird. It was very strong, the thing I was noticing, but I couldn't quite think what it was, how to describe it. These people on the talk show—there was something the same about them, something special that I didn't like. What was it? I was very excited. Stuff from the zoo was flashing through my mind. I thought about the lesser kudu. I could see her beautiful brown eyes. I wanted to cry, I loved her so much. On the talk show they were wheeling out a watermelon cut in half and filled with shredded carrots, and there were little American flags on it. Pod people! The movie! It was a true movie! There were real pod people. I smelled the tiger. I heard the lizard band. Tears were rolling off my chin. We had been invaded by the pod people. It wasn't all clear yet. I didn't know what this had to do with the Chicken Man—or with me. But I just knew that somehow the whole thing was connected. I couldn't hear the sound of the TV screen anymore. My ears were filled with lizard music. The credits on the talk show were coming down, and the people who had been on the show were pretending to shake hands.

54

I wondered why I was sobbing. I didn't feel sad, and the sobbing seemed to be going on by itself—in another room, or somewhere away from me. I was trying to pull myself together, but I was together. I had a feeling that this was all leading somewhere, and I was happy about it. But this was serious. Pod people were no joke. I felt myself calming down. I wondered why I wasn't worried. Nothing like this had ever happened to me, and you don't discover that you've been invaded by the pod people every day. I was feeling very certain about all sorts of things that I didn't really understand. One thing I was certain about—not everybody was pod people. There were pod people—and what? Lizards! The lizards were not podish at all. The Chicken Man was unpod. Shane Fergussen was no pod. I wasn't. Mom and Dad weren't. Leslie definitely was. I couldn't make up my mind about Walter. I hoped he wasn't.

I spent a long time thinking about people I knew—pod or not pod. Most of them were. The late movie was the one about the guy in the marines who is a coward all through boot camp, and then he has a talk with the old sergeant, who turns out to be his father or something, and he's a hero in the war. Just as well—I couldn't have enjoyed anything good. I was waiting up for the lizards and my phone call to the Chicken Man.

The lizards came on right after the late movie. The music was great. I flipped the knob, and sure enough, they were on every channel, just as I thought. It was hard to tear myself away from the set and dial the number. When the receiver picked up on the other end, I could hear lizard music coming through the phone. It sounded good. For some reason I thought of hot soup.

"Fergussen's Confectionery," I heard.

"Mr. Fergussen, this is Victor," I said. "Is the Chicken Man there?"

"Never heard of him," Shane Fergussen said. "Hold the line." I held.

Then a voice. "Milo Schtunk, here. To whom am I addressed?"

"This is Victor," I said. "Is this the Chicken Man?"

"How should I know?" the voice said. "You just said it was Victor."

"I mean, am *I* talking *to* the Chicken Man?" I shouted.

"You are talking to Peter Breughel the Elder, known to some as the C.M.," the voice said.

"I'm Victor, the kid you've been following around," I said.

"My man! Victor, how are you?"

"Mixed up, sort of," I said. "I've been trying to get in touch with you. I want to make an appointment."

"Fine. Come to my office tomorrow," said Peter Breughel the Elder, also known as Milo Schtunk, a.k.a. Charles Swan, Hubert Van Eyck, Matthias Grunewald, Lucas Cranach, Jr., Herr Doktor Professor Horace Kupeckie, Plt.D.

"Where's that," I said.

"Umm, what's tomorrow, Wednesday? Try the Reptile House, Hogboro Zoo, in the late A.M."

"I'll be there," I said. "By the way, how much do you charge?"

"That depends on what you want done."

"I want some things explained," I said.

"No charge for explanations," the Chicken Man said. "However, there is a charge for guiding. I'm a licensed guide."

"What?" I said. *Buzzzz*—he had hung up.

I finally got to see the end of the lizard show. They just finished playing and left—packed up their instruments and walked off, carrying the little black musical instrument cases. Then the camera showed the empty chairs for a long time.

I guessed it was time to go to bed. I had a lot to do in the A.M., as the Chicken Man said.

"It's time to play You Bet Your Duck!" a voice said. I jumped. It was coming from the TV set. The picture was still the empty chairs. "Yes, friends,

57

You Bet Your Duck, the exciting lizard quiz!" The picture had changed. There was a lizard wearing a Donald Duck mask! "And here's your old friend, the genial quizmaster, the Inept Eft!" the lizard announcer in the duck mask said. Another lizard in a duck mask came onto the screen. He was smoking a cigar through the mask. "Welcome, welcome to 'You Bet Your Duck,'" the Inept Eft said, "and now, let's meet our first two contestants." Two more lizards wearing duck masks came out. The Inept Eft asked them their names.

"Jim and Linda Lacerta," they said. It was interesting listening to lizards talk. They sounded perfectly normal. Up to now, I had only heard them play musical instruments.

"As you know, every correct answer is worth 75,000 Agama Dollars," the Inept Eft said. "Twelve wrong answers in a row, and you lose the game." I wondered what an Agama Dollar was. "And now it's time to play You Bet Your Duck," the quizmaster said. "The first question is, Who invented the telephone?"

Jim and Linda Lacerta sort of whispered to each other. Then they turned to the Inept Eft. "Was it Salamander Graham Bell?"

"Correct, for 75,000 Agama Dollars!" the Eft shouted. "Next question. Name a famous Spanish painter who was a lizard."

Jim and Linda whispered again. They were still whispering when the bell rang.

"I'm sorry, there goes the bell," the Eft said. "The correct answer is El Gecko. Remember,

58

eleven more wrong answers in a row, and you lose the game. The next question is, Name the lizard who conquered the ancient world."

Jim and Linda went back to whispering.

"Come on, now, this should be easy after the first question," the Eft said.

"Salamander the Great!" they both shouted at once.

"Right, for 150,000 Agama Dollars!" the Eft shouted. The audience was clapping. I wondered why they all wore duck masks. I was getting a little bored—and tired. Except that everyone was a lizard wearing a duck mask, and speaking English, it was just a regular quiz show.

"'Red Scales in the Sunset' is correct for 225,000 Agama Dollars!" the Eft was shouting. I wondered how many lizard programs were on late at night. I was starting to doze off with my chin on my fist. Every now and then it would slip off, and I would wake up suddenly.

"I'm sorry, you should have known that. The answer is Newt Rockne," the Eft said. My eyes were burning. My head was nodding.

"She said, 'Iguana be alone,'" Jim and Linda said.

"Kee-rect, for 375,000 Agama Dollars!" the Eft said. I got to my feet. I felt as though I were walking on the bottom of a lake. My feet were like lead.

"I'm sorry, it's the Emperor Max Chameleon—" *Click!* I turned off the set and dragged myself to my room. I hadn't slept in my bed for two nights, and it felt great when I got in. I could still sort of hear the Inept Eft in my head. "Elizardbeth Taylor is right for a half million Agama Dollars!" I was asleep in five seconds.

"Victor, wake up!" It was my mother. "Wake up! It's ten o'clock!" What was she doing here? I was having a hard time waking up. I was holding something heavy and hard in my hand—the telephone! I had answered the telephone in my sleep. "Victor! Victor! Are you all right? You were saying something about ducks."

I was trying to get myself together. "Everything's fine, Mom," I said. "Leslie let me stay up and watch the late movie, and I overslept." I felt myself getting things back under control.

"A fine thing," my mother said, "letting a ten-year-old boy—"

"Eleven," I said.

"—an eleven-year-old boy stay up till all hours. I'm going to call her at the office and give her a good talking to."

I imagined that horn that goes off in submarine movies just before they make an emergency dive.

HONK HONK DIVE! DIVE! I had to think fast. "Well, you see there was this boy here—someone Leslie knows—and he's sort of like a hippie, and Leslie told me she didn't want me to go to bed until he went home."

"Oh, well—" Mom was thinking. "What's this boy's name?"

"Hubert Van Eyck," I said.

"Is he a nice boy?"

"No, he's dumb. Leslie didn't like him. She said that she never gets to go on a date, and when someone finally asks her, he turns out to be a creep. She's in a bad mood."

"Oh, I see," Mom said. I liked the way she said it. She had heard this routine from Leslie plenty of times, and it always went on for hours with Leslie whining and repeating herself over and over. I was just about certain she wasn't going to risk calling Leslie for a few days, and certainly not at the office. Leslie would have gone into her act at work without a second thought. She doesn't care where she is when she makes a scene.

"Well, is everything okay?" Depth bomb attack over. I told Mom how everything was fine and asked how they were enjoying their vacation. As I suspected, Mom went on about scenery for a while. I told her it sounded fine. Then she went guilty, and started in on how there wasn't all that much to do, and she hadn't seen any kids my age, and how I probably wouldn't have enjoyed it. I told her I thought so too and I had to go meet a friend.

61

I got dressed fast, grabbed a Twinkie to eat on the way, and ran for the bus. It was lucky my mother had called. As it was, I was afraid I was going to be too late and miss the Chicken Man. For a few seconds, before I woke all the way up, I was sort of scared that my mother had come back from her trip, or that she'd never gone, and it had all been a dream—the lizards and the Chicken Man and everything. I realized that I was enjoying all this very much. Even if the planet had been invaded by the pods, maybe there was something I could do about it, like that guy in the movie who was going to save the world. I would have hated it if it all turned out to be a dream. I was having a great adventure. I munched on my Twinkie, and felt good about everything.

The bus rolled into the terminal, and I grabbed a special zoo bus. I was still sucking a piece of Twinkie out of my teeth when I got off in front of the Hogboro Zoo. I guessed it was maybe 10:45. I really needed a big pocket watch. Shane Fergussen had some in his store for $2.98; I never knew watches were so cheap. I made a note: Buy watch. There was a big sign right inside the zoo with a map of the place and arrows pointing in all directions with animals painted on them. One had a lizard on it. I went off in the direction it pointed.

The Reptile House was another of those big brick buildings. Over the door it said Reptile House with a couple of lizards carved on both sides. I had certainly seen a lot of lizards lately. I was getting so I could tell a lizard that was good-looking from one that wasn't—by lizard standards, I mean. The ones carved on the Reptile House were good-looking lizards. I went inside.

It was dark inside the Reptile House. There wasn't any smell. It was quiet. There wasn't anybody there, just a zoo guard standing near the entrance. All around the walls were glass windows with green plants behind them. It was cool—cool and dark and quiet. The windows had lights behind them shining on the plants. They looked like TV screens and the windows in the empty store where I had seen the album cover. Every now and then a little green head moved behind one of the windows. It was so quiet in the Reptile House that I could hear myself breathe. I just stood in the doorway for a while until my breathing got quiet. Then I went farther inside.

Over each window there was a little card that told about the reptiles inside. The first thing I saw was an anaconda. Anacondas are the biggest snakes in the world; they get to be over thirty feet long! The one at the Hogboro Zoo is twenty-two feet. He was just lying in his cage, doubled back on himself—folded like a hairpin. The cage wasn't long enough for him to stretch all the way out. He wasn't moving, just breathing. I looked at him. He looked at me. At least I think he looked at me—it was hard to tell. He looked sort of intelligent—for a snake. The anaconda lifted his head for a while, then he laid it down.

"Well, Mr. Anaconda, you may be very big, but you're not very interesting," I thought.

"Who cares what you think," the anaconda said. He didn't really say it—he just looked as though that's what he'd say.

They have mostly snakes in the Reptile House, not so many lizards at all. One snake I liked was called the emerald tree boa. It looked a little like the anaconda, only much smaller, and was a beautiful green color. There were cobras—sort of scary. They really do spread out their hoods like they are always shown doing in jungle movies. There were black and green mambas, rattlesnakes, and copperheads—all poisonous. There are only a couple of poisonous lizards, it said on a card over the Gila monster's cage. I felt good about that.

My favorite animal in the whole place was the chameleon. It was really a weird-looking lizard, sort of humpbacked, with a tail that curls up in a little spiral. Chameleons can change color! Not only that, but they have these great eyes. Each eye sort of sticks out at the top of a little bump, and they can rotate their eyes in all different directions, together or separately. They're funny looking, and sort of friendly looking too. I thought that I might like to have one as a pet. It said on the card that they make good pets.

I spent a long time watching the chameleons. They changed color a couple of times—and they have this great slow-motion way of moving. I really enjoyed them. A fly got into the chameleon cage, and one of the chameleons shot out this incredibly long tongue, and just sort of zooped it right into his mouth. They have these great little hands and feet.

Chameleons are terrific lizards. They have a lot of personality. Lizards in general are friendlier than snakes. Most snakes either look mean, or look like they couldn't care less.

It occurred to me that I had been in the Reptile House for a long time. Almost nobody had come in—maybe two or three people had come in and said. "Oooo, look at the snakes," and left after a few minutes. I must have been in the Reptile House for two hours.

Where was the Chicken Man? Had I missed him? I was getting tired of standing around in the dark, looking at reptiles. I went over to have another look at the alligators. They were in a sort of open pit at the end of the building. There wasn't any glass in front of them. There was a little fence about four feet high, and on the other side was this pit with water in the bottom, and some rocks and plants. The alligators were just hanging around—watching me. I wondered what they'd do if I fell into the pit.

"If you fell into that pit, they'd gobble you up in two seconds flat," someone said. I looked around. The zoo guard was standing nearby. He had a green uniform, like a police uniform, and a badge that said Zoo Police. He also had one of those rectangular black plastic nameplates with his name on it in white letters. Anton Anolis.

"Did you speak to me?" I asked.

"I was just observing that the alligators have no manners at all," Anton Anolis said. "Most of the reptiles, even the real poisonous ones, will treat you just fine if you are polite. Those alligators would eat anyone. They'd eat the President of the United States if he fell into that pit, which is why I hope he never comes here."

"Did they ever actually eat anyone?" I asked.

"Well, not that I know of, but I dropped my lunch down there by accident once, and it was gone in a flash—two salami sandwiches, a tangerine, and a jelly doughnut—snapped up by one of those monsters. Then there used to be a keeper named Jones who vanished without a trace—never heard of him again. Some people say that the alligators were smiling for a week after that. Maybe he got eaten, maybe he didn't. I kept an eye on the alligator pit for maybe a shoe, or a zoo badge, but I never found anything. I guess you're really interested in reptiles," Anton Anolis said.

"I am sort of getting interested in them," I said, "but the reason I've been here for such a long time is that I'm waiting for a friend. You don't know anything about someone called the Chicken Man, do you?"

"The Chicken Man?" Anton Anolis said. "Never heard of him. Come this way." Anton led me to a side door of the Reptile House. The door opened onto a little sort of courtyard with trees and benches. Sitting on one of the benches reading a newspaper was the Chicken Man. It wasn't a regular newspaper; it was in some foreign language with a different alphabet. The letters were funny-looking loopy things with thick and thin parts, and the Chicken Man was turning the pages backwards. He saw me and folded the newspaper.

"Ah, Victor! Glad to see you. Come and sit down," the Chicken Man said. I sat down on the bench.

"I see you've been enjoying a visit with the reptiles," he said. "I never go in there anymore, ever since poor Jones disappeared." The Chicken Man looked off into the distance. He seemed to be thinking about something. He didn't say anything for a long time. I sat there, keeping quiet. I was getting uncomfortable.

"How's Claudia?" I said finally.

"Ask her yourself," the Chicken Man said. He took off his hat, and there was Claudia—sleeping. She opened one red eye, gave me a cluck, and settled back to sleep. The Chicken Man put his hat over her again.

"Now, what in particular did you want to see me about?" the Chicken Man asked.

"I'm not sure why, but I think you can answer a lot of questions that have begun to bother me," I said.

"Very likely," said the Chicken Man. "Such as—"

"Such as, where are the lizard programs on television coming from? Such as, why did you make that lizard appear in your hand the other day? Such as—"

"Wait a minute, wait a minute," the Chicken Man said. "Just hold the thought for a minute while I get set up here." The Chicken Man dug around in his raincoat and came up with a huge pipe, a curved one. He stuffed it full of tobacco, struck a match on the sole of his shoe, and lit it, making huge clouds of blue smoke.

"A bowl of Latakia always helps me listen, and I perceive that you have a complicated problem. Proceed, Victor," the Chicken Man said. I had sort of forgotten where I was in my questions, watching the Chicken Man light the big pipe.

"I have some notes here," I said. I got out my notebook. "By the way, what *is* your name? I've heard about fifteen names for you so far."

"It's true, I am known by a variety of names," the Chicken Man said. "Which one do you like best?"

"Charles Swan," I said.

"Call me Charlie," the Chicken Man said.

"It was you in the taxi, wasn't it?" I asked.

"Sure, you knew that, didn't you?" Charlie said.

It was hard to keep a conversation going in one direction. The Chicken Man, Charlie, had a way of getting me off the track. "Now, about the lizards," I said.

"Oh yes, did you have a look at the iguana in there?" Charlie pointed his pipe at the Reptile House. "They have a fine double-crested basilisk. Quite rare, really."

"Was that the one that runs around on its hind legs?" I asked.

Charlie was doing it again. "Yes, that's the one—interesting family, the iguana." Charlie puffed on his pipe.

There was another silence. It was frustrating. Charlie was real good at taking control of a conversation, and then he'd just let it die out. I wondered if he was charging me for all his pipe smoking, and stuff about iguanas, but I was embarrassed to ask him. It all reminded me of the chameleons walking in slow motion on their little branch.

"We've been invaded by people from another planet!" I shouted.

"Not people—creatures," Charlie said.

⧈⧈

"**W**ill you please tell me what's going on?" I screamed. "I'm only eleven years old, and some of this stuff has got me very upset!"

"There's no need to get excited, Victor," Charlie said. "Now just tell me what's on your mind."

"Lizards," I said. "Lizards are on my mind, and pod people, and you—you've been turning up everywhere!"

"I know quite a lot about the lizards," Charlie said, "somewhat less about the pod people as you call them. As to me turning up everywhere, I've always done that. It's you who have taken to turning up lately. We were certain to meet once you started that."

"Well, if you know so much, why aren't you excited, or at least worried?" I asked. I hadn't been bothered too much by the thought of the pod people invading the earth until that moment. "Don't the pod people worry you?"

"If you mean the pod people in that old science-fiction movie, they don't worry me at all," Charlie said. "Worrying about them is a good way to become one."

"I thought they came from outer space," I said.

"No, not the pods—it's the other ones who come from outer space," Charlie said.

"The other ones—do you mean the lizards?" I asked.

"In a way—in a way the lizards are from outer space," Charlie said. "I see you're a little confused about this stuff."

"I'm only eleven," I said.

"Quite so," Charlie said. "I will try my best to explain it to you, as well as I understand it myself. But first, I suggest we stop at the refreshment stand for a bite of something nutritious. It's almost two o'clock, and I expect we're both hungry." There was no way to hurry Charlie. He said that he didn't believe that people should talk about serious things while they were eating, so I had to listen to him carry on about the differences among various old violins while he put away six hot dogs. I had a hot dog myself, and a root beer.

Charlie suggested we take a walk around the zoo while we talked. "I gather you've only recently noticed the lizard programs on television," Charlie said.

"Well, I don't usually get to stay up late," I said. "They've been on every night so far since I've been staying up."

"And you observed that there was nothing about them in the daily television listings?"

"Yes," I said.

"Perhaps you even called the TV station to inquire," Charlie went on.

"I did that," I said, "and they didn't tell me anything."

"Not surprising," said Charlie. "They don't know anything. Now, what's this about pod people?"

"Last night I began to notice that there were these people on television—regular television—before the lizard programs. They aren't regular humans—it's hard to explain—something about them doesn't make sense. They seem to—they seem to—"

Charlie finished the thought for me. "They seem to be going through the motions of being humans without really meaning it or understanding it."

"That's it," I said. "They're real, but they're not. It got me thinking about this movie where pods from space come down, and replicas of the real people come out and replace everyone."

"I've seen the movie," Charlie said. "Everyone has. It's an excellent film, but not entirely accurate. You see, the pod people, as you like to call them, are not from another planet. They are ordinary people who have developed in a certain way. It can happen to anyone, if they're unlucky."

"That's even scarier than being invaded from space," I said. I thought about the stupid people on the talk show. I was worried that it could happen to me. It had happened to my sister.

"What makes people get that way?" I asked.

"Nobody seems to know," Charlie said. "There's a lot of it going around. My personal belief is that it comes from eating too much prepackaged food, but that's just a little theory of mine."

"It's a serious problem, isn't it?" I asked.

"Oh yes, it's a problem, but it doesn't do to worry about it too much. Somehow, people who get all concerned about podism usually seem to wind up catching it." Charlie's voice was trailing off. He was looking at the rhinoceros. "You know, the white rhino isn't white at all. He's a grayish color like any other rhinoceros," Charlie was saying. He was off again. "The term 'white' is derived from the Afrikaans word *weit* or 'wide,' having to do with the wide or squarish shape of the lip, thus distinguishing the white rhino from the black rhino, which isn't black but gray and has a pointed or prehensile upper lip."

"What about the lizards?" I asked. You just have to ignore it when Charlie gets off the subject.

"Umm? What's that?" Charlie asked.

"The lizards," I said. "You said that the lizards come from outer space."

"In a way, in a way they do. It might be more proper to say they come from *other* space."

I was having a hard time making any sense out of what Charlie was saying. "Are you explaining or guiding?" I asked.

"Explaining. Why?" Charlie asked.

"I just wanted to know if I was going to have to pay for any of this," I said.

"No, no, as I told you, there is no charge for explanations. However, there is a charge for guiding. I'm a licensed guide," Charlie said. "Does this mean that you're ready to start out?"

"Start out? Where to?" I asked.

"To find the lizards," Charlie said.

"How much will it cost?" I asked. I was pretty sure that the explanations had gone about as far as they were going to go.

"Two-fifty per day—you bring your own lunch," Charlie said.

"Let's go," I said.

Charlie looked at his watch. "It's almost five o'clock. Claudia and I have a show to do on the Clark Street bus. I'll meet you in the A.M. at Shane Fergussen's candy store," Charlie said. With that Charlie took off. He had a kind of sideways style of running.

There was nothing to do but go home and wait for the A.M. The zoo was about to close anyway. The McDonaldsville bus was crowded with commuters coming home from work. When I got home there were two postcards in the mailbox, one from Mom and Dad and one from Leslie. They were both about the same—having fun, wish you were here, etc.—except that Leslie's card also said, "If you ever tell, I'll kill you."

I had some time before the news. I thought about what to have for supper. I looked in the freezer. The neat rows of TV dinners in boxes turned me off. I thought about what Charlie had said. I didn't really understand what he meant by prepackaged food, and I couldn't see what that could have to do with pod people. Still it sort of spoiled my appetite for those TV dinners. I thought about something not prepackaged to eat. I had already done the egg thing. The frying pan was still soaking to get some of the black off. I didn't feel like cooking again.

I was looking around the kitchen, thinking about what to have for supper, when I noticed the calendar from the Pizza Palace. Every so often my family orders a pizza from the Pizza Palace. They bring it right to the house. The only thing is, nobody in my family likes anchovies. I mean, they hate anchovies. Not one of them can even stand to look at an anchovy. It makes them sick if they even think there's an anchovy in the same room with them. I love anchovies. I don't know how I found out about them—it sure wasn't at home. Now, there is nothing to prevent ordering a pizza from the Pizza Palace and telling the man that you only want anchovies on half the pizza, or a quarter of the pizza. We do that with sausage because we all like it except Leslie. Of course she doesn't hate sausage—I mean she doesn't want to have a war against sausages. She just doesn't care to have sausage on her pizza. It's perfectly reasonable. She doesn't want sausage, she doesn't have to eat sausage. As I understand it, that's why America is a great country. Nobody has to eat sausage if they don't want to. But anchovies are a different story. Especially Leslie, but Mom and Dad too, *freak out* about anchovies. They won't let me eat them in their presence. Even if I were to take my special anchovy slices of pizza away and eat them in another room, Leslie would start screaming that she could taste anchovies in her pizza and gagging and carrying on. Therefore I almost never get to have pizza with anchovies, although I am an American too.

I called the Pizza Palace and ordered a pizza with double anchovies. I switched on the TV and sat down to wait for my pizza. I had already checked the icebox—there was plenty of milk. That's another thing they can't stand. I like milk with my anchovy pizza. They won't even let me talk about it. The only time I ever get it is when I am over at Howard Foster's house. I have rights, just like anybody else.

The quiz program, the one where the people climb out of a greased pit with a mouthful of money, was just ending. The announcer was telling how they spray the money with Lysol at the beginning of each show so the contestants won't get sick from the germs on the money. The doorbell rang—that didn't take long. I went to the door. There was Charlie! He was carrying a big cardboard pizza box.

"Hey, Victor!" he said. "Is this where you live?" Apparently Charlie delivered pizzas part-time. He handed me the box. "Anchovies, ugh!" he said. "That will be three dollars." I paid him. "I've got to run—lots of pizzas to deliver," Charlie said. "Are we still meeting at Fergussen's place in the A.M.?"

"Sure," I said.

"See you then. By the way, don't miss the late movie—it's a good one." He was gone.

76

I checked the TV listings. The late movie was *Invasion of the Fat Men.* It did sound interesting. The bell rang again. It was Charlie.

"I almost forgot to tell you—bring a bathing suit, and a big plastic garbage bag, and some strong twine." Then he was off again.

Bathing suit? Garbage bag? Twine? I didn't understand any of this. I sat down again. The Roger Mudd show had already started. My pizza was cooling on the kitchen table. You can never trust a pizza until it is really good and cold. A pizza that only seems warm to the touch can still give a serious pizza burn. Hot pockets of molten cheese are lurking under the surface. The smart way to eat a pizza is to give it at least twenty minutes to cool off before you put your teeth into it. Some people never learn this. My sister, Leslie, for example—there's no point in someone like her eating a pizza, because she's always in pain after the first bite.

Roger Mudd was talking about the President—he had a cold, and had decided to stay indoors. I went to test my pizza. It seemed okay. Roger said that they were going to bring back the two-dollar bill. A poor news day, obviously. Sometimes they really have to stretch to fill up a half hour. Walter is really good at that. I remember when those guys went to the moon, Walter could talk for half an hour about nothing. I really miss him sometimes when he's on vacation.

The news ended. I ate my pizza and watched a game show. It was the one where people get all dressed up in funny costumes and make fools of themselves. The ones in the funniest costumes get to be on the program and get asked easy questions, which half of them miss.

I rummaged around in the kitchen for some twine and a garbage bag. I found the things I needed and put them in a paper bag, along with some peanut butter sandwiches, and put the bag on the table near the front door, next to the stack of phony letters to Mom and Dad.

I got through another evening of prime-time television. I don't know why all the good stuff isn't on until late at night. I finished my model—all but the painting—and cleaned up the newspapers and stuff. I always paint models in the basement, because Mom says the smell of the paint lingers for days. I think it smells pretty good. I felt sort of bored and restless. I wanted the evening to be over so it would be night. I wanted it to be tomorrow so I could go with Charlie, wherever it was we were going.

Invasion of the Fat Men was a good movie. In the movie, some scientists notice thousands of round things like meteorites descending to the earth, only they descend very slowly. People are watching through telescopes. As the round things get closer, people can see that they are not meteorites—they are fat men in sports coats, with checked trousers and two-tone shoes with rubber soles, and knitted neckties—and they are floating down to earth like big round snowflakes. There is a worldwide panic. It takes days for the fat men to float down.

When the fat men start alighting on earth, everyone has been a nervous wreck for days. Each fat man weighs about six hundred pounds, and there are millions and millions of them, so there's no point in trying to resist them if they are unfriendly. The governments of the various countries just hope they can negotiate with them. All the presidents and kings and so forth are waiting for leaders of the fat men to contact them. They never do. They just start looking around for places to eat. They especially like hamburger stands and pizzerias and places like that. Most of the fat men from space go to California and New Jersey, because they have the most drive-ins, but the fat men are all over the world and still descending. It's like a blizzard of fat men from space. No airplanes can fly because of the ones floating down, and no cars or trains or buses can go very far without getting snarled up in crowds of fat men from space strolling along eating Twinkies and chocolate Mallomars. The whole planet is covered with pizza crusts and hamburger wrappers. It is almost impossible to walk in the streets of the cities because of all the empty Dixie cups and crowds of fat men. The earth people can get nothing to eat but fruits and vegetables, lean meats and rye toast—the only things the fat men from space don't eat. Civilization as we know it is coming to an end.

In the Rocky Mountains, in a secret underground laboratory, scientists bake a huge jelly doughnut. They use the last fifty million tons of sugar on earth that the fat men have not taken control of. Then they catapult the jelly doughnut into outer space, beyond the earth's gravitational pull. The fat men notice the jelly doughnut and take off after it. The last scene is Newark, New Jersey, covered with popsicle sticks and empty cellophane wrappers from Devil Dogs. The people come out of their houses and watch the last of the fat men floating upward. Then someone says, "Do you suppose they're gone for good?" and someone else says, "We must always be prepared. Never again shall earth be taken by surprise without an arsenal of jelly doughnuts."

A pretty good movie, I thought, if a little weird. The lizards appeared on schedule, but tonight the reception wasn't very good. There were all those little dots jumping, like when there's no signal coming from the station, and you could just make out the lizards behind the dots. The sound wasn't too good either. It was just as well—I really needed to get to sleep at a decent hour if I wanted to be fresh for my adventure in the morning.

In the morning, I woke up early enough to take a shower. I hadn't had time for one the past few days, and I was starting to get sort of grimy. I put on my bathing trunks under my clothes, picked up the bag with the lunch, twine, and so forth, picked up a forgery to mail, and went to the bus stop. I didn't bother with breakfast, because I was planning to have something to eat at Shane Fergussen's candy store.

12

I was sitting at the counter of Shane Fergussen's candy store having a grape soda and a jelly doughnut for breakfast, when Charlie walked in.

"That looks good," he said. "I'll have the same, Shane." I looked at my new $2.98 watch—it was 9:45. The bus from McDonaldsville had been crowded with commuters. "A grape soda and a jelly doughnut for my good friend Albrecht Dürer," Shane Fergussen said.

"I thought your name was Charlie," I said to the Chicken Man.

"—or Charlie for short," Shane Fergussen said.

Charlie had a big bag with him. It was made out of some kind of rough cloth. "You're a good swimmer, aren't you Victor?" he asked.

"Sure," I said.

"Do you like boats?"

I wasn't sure—I had never actually been in a boat. I said I supposed I like them.

"Fine, because we're going for a boat ride today," Charlie said. We paid Shane Fergussen and left the candy store. It was 9:58.

"What boat ride?" I asked.

"Out to the middle of Lake Mishagoo," Charlie said.

Lake Mishagoo is this big lake that Hogboro is right next to. It's not just some little pond. You can't see to the other side of it, and it gets pretty choppy sometimes. Mishagoo is an Indian word. It means "lake-so-big-you-can't-see-the-other-side." That's the sort of thing they teach us in school.

It was just a few blocks to the lake. Charlie was carrying the big bag over his shoulder. It looked heavy. He was wearing his hat, so I assumed that Claudia was under it. Charlie didn't say anything; he just puffed along carrying the bag. When we came to an intersection, he'd set the bag down and wipe his face with a handkerchief.

"Do you want me to help you carry that?" I asked.

"The guide carries the bag," Charlie said.

To get to the lake you cross a street, and there's a little park. The park stretches along the lakefront, and in some places there are beaches. In between the beaches are stretches of rocks along the shore. We wound up on some rocks.

"The lake! The lake! We made it!" Charlie said. This struck me as weird—we'd only gone about eight blocks from Shane Fergussen's candy store.

"Where's the boat?" I asked.

"Wait," Charlie said. Out of the big bag he dumped a big shapeless yellow thing. He spread the yellow thing out on the rocks. It was shaped sort of like a flat bathtub; it was made of something like rubber. Charlie found a valve and started blowing into it. It was one of those war surplus, blow-up life rafts. As it inflated, it looked more like an out-of-shape doughnut than a bathtub. The doughnut part was what got filled with air. There was a rubber floor, and Charlie dug a pair of collapsible oars out of the bag.

"Our yacht," he said, when he had finished blowing it up.

"Where are we supposed to go in that thing?" I asked. I wasn't too sure I wanted to ride in it. Charlie had set the little boat in the water, and it was bobbing around.

"Just hop in—I'll tell you all about it on the way," he said.

I hopped in. "Start telling me now, so we can go back to shore if I don't like it." Charlie had taken his hat off. Claudia was there all right. She spread her wings like the eagle on a half-dollar. Charlie was paddling with one of the collapsible oars.

"We are going to Invisible Island, over there!" He gestured with his oar.

"I don't see any island," I said.

"Hence the name," Charlie said. "It's there all right, and a very interesting island it is, too. Now grab an oar and do some work while I tell you about it. The guide doesn't have to do *all* the work." I grabbed an oar. Claudia had hopped off Charlie's head and was standing in the front of the raft. She still had her wings spread out and her beak thrust forward, like a figurehead on an old-fashioned sailing ship.

"Invisible Island is a volcanic island, fairly large, that has broken off from the bottom and floats around in Lake Mishagoo," Charlie said. "It has been floating around for millions of years, but it never floats any closer to shore than fifteen or twenty miles. Just now it is rather close to Hogboro."

"Why is it called Invisible?" I asked.

"Because it is invisible," Charlie said. "You should have known that."

"I should have," I said. "Let me put it another way. Why is it invisible?"

"I was just coming to that," Charlie said. "It's fairly complicated. You see, Invisible Island has the quality of bending rays, such as rays of light. You know that light rays tend to travel in more or less straight lines, but they can be bent. Well, certain islands bend them a lot. If you look straight at Invisible Island, you don't see the island, you see *around* the island, and you think you're looking directly at whatever's on the other side. Also, if you sail straight at the island, you will simply sail around it, thinking you're going in a straight line. It isn't easy to explain—there's a book called *Mount Analogue* by René Daumal that tells all about it. Just take my word for it. We are paddling directly toward a very large island, bigger than the city of Hogboro, and it's only about twelve miles off."

"If you can't see it, how do you know for sure?" I asked.

"I don't," Charlie said, "but Claudia does. Chickens have an uncanny sense of direction. The only problem is getting them to take you where you want to go."

"Then Claudia is—" I started to say.

"That's right. Claudia is navigating." Charlie said.

"But if the island bends things so they go around it—" I got stuck.

Charlie helped me out. "It's a force field—like an invisible wall."

"Well then, how are we going to get onto the island?" I asked.

"We have a long way to paddle yet," Charlie said. "How about a canoeing song to pass the time?" With that he began to sing some song about bright paddles and good comrades and stuff like that. He kept it up for about an hour. Claudia continued to point the way with her beak. I was getting into the rhythm of the paddling. I liked the little rubber boat and the feeling of being on the lake. The water made a nice sound slapping the sides of the boat. Charlie paddled with a long sweeping motion. After a while he laid his oar across the little boat. "Lunchtime," he said. I looked at my watch, 11:43. I got out my peanut butter sandwiches. Charlie and Claudia had brought tuna fish.

I hadn't forgotten my question. "How do we get past the force field, or invisible barrier, or whatever it is?" I asked.

Charlie swallowed a mouthful of tuna fish sandwich. "Very easy—we go under it. That's what the waterproof bag is for. We put our clothes in there, tie the bag to an ankle, and just swim under. Once we're inside the barrier, it's just a few hundred feet to the shore."

"What about Claudia?" I asked. "Will she swim under the barrier too?"

"No, unfortunately Claudia gets sinus headaches from swimming underwater. Claudia will stay with the boat and wait for us to come back," Charlie said.

"The lizards live on the island, right?" I asked.

"Right," Charlie said. "The reason you've been getting the TV pictures lately is that the island has floated very close to shore, and the weather has been just right. Their TV signal bounces off low clouds and hits McDonaldsville and Hogboro."

"Doesn't the force field stop the TV signal?" I asked.

"It's all around them, not over them," Charlie said. "If it were on top of them, they wouldn't get any sunlight. That stands to reason, doesn't it?" I agreed that it did. It had been some time since I had wondered if Charlie were crazy. I spent most of the next couple of hours doing that, as we paddled along, following Claudia's beak. I noticed that she would change direction every now and then, and Charlie would change the direction of the boat. I decided to say nothing about it.

Claudia started clucking and jumping up and down. Charlie threw out the anchor, which consisted of a sort of cloth bucket on a long cord. "This is it," he said. We were in the middle of nowhere— we couldn't even see the shore. Once in a while, when the boat bobbed up, I could see the tallest buildings in Hogboro. The rest of the time there was nothing but water in every direction.

"Let's get our clothes off and into the garbage bag," Charlie said. Claudia, who had been clucking and jumping and pointing her wings in one direction, was now clucking and jumping and pointing in another.

"Wait a minute!" I shouted. "I'm not getting out of this boat!"

"If you don't get out of the boat, how are you going to get onto the island?" Charlie asked.

"What island? I don't see any island! All I see is water and some crazy chicken who is pointing like a hunting dog in three different directions."

"There's no need to insult Claudia, after all the work she did in bringing us here," Charlie said. "Besides, I don't see what you're so worried about. I'm taking all the responsibility. If anything were to happen to you, I'd lose my guide's license."

I was getting hysterical. "What license? What guide's license are you talking about? I never heard of a licensed guide, except maybe in the Maine woods."

"This is a funny time to get technical," Charlie said, "but if you insist—" Charlie dug out an old wallet and fished around in it. He came up with a card and handed it to me. "My credentials," he said. The card was black on one side, with a sort of compass printed in gold. The other side was light blue, with a white outline of a map of the United States. Printed in big yellow letters, it said:

CAPTAIN MOONFLIGHT'S
Secret Squadron
This is to certify that:
<u>VINCENT VAN GOGH</u>
is a licensed guide.

"What does this mean?" I screamed. "What's Captain Moonflight? Who's Vincent Van Gogh? What am I doing out here in the middle of a lake with a crazy old man and a chicken?" I started to cry.

"Guides are trained to deal with panic," Charlie said. "You really ought to trust me and start getting ready to swim. The way I figure it, we only have about three minutes before the boat sinks."

"*Sinks?*" I was really in bad shape. I had let a crazy man row me out to the middle of a lake where there was supposed to be an invisible island. I had just gone along with the whole game, and now I was going to die. "*Sinks? What are you talking about?*"

"Just be quiet for a second and listen," Charlie said. I listened—there was a steady hissing noise. Claudia had punched a lot of holes in the rubber boat when she was jumping up and down.

"I really should have put little boots on Claudia before we started out," Charlie said. "Now she's going to get a terrible headache from swimming underwater."

"Charlie, do you swear there's an island?" I asked.

"Of course I do. Now get your clothes in this garbage bag before they get soaked," he said. Charlie had stripped off his clothes and was stuffing them into the bag. He had on one of those old-fashioned bathing suits that comes down to the knees and elbows. It was red and white stripes.

The boat was getting sort of soft and lumpy-looking. I struggled out of my clothes and put them in the bag. "You promise there's an island?"

"Official guide's word of honor," Charlie said. He had squeezed all the air out of the plastic bag and tied the neck tightly with the twine. He was tying the other end of the twine around his ankle. There was water in the boat. Claudia was looking disgusted.

"Chickens hate to swim," Charlie said, "but it won't be far."

"Which way do we go?" I asked. I was still sure I was going to die.

"Just follow Claudia. She'll make for land like a bandit," Charlie said. We were sitting in water. Then the boat just slid away under us, and we were swimming. I couldn't see Claudia.

"Dive! Dive!" Charlie shouted. Then he was gone too.

I looked around—nothing but water. The horrible thought came to me that Charlie couldn't swim. Crazy as he was, he might not have thought of it. Of course, chickens can't swim, and Claudia had probably gone to the bottom like a stone. For some strange reason, I thought of my new $2.98 pocket watch ticking away in the waterproof bag, attached to the ankle of the drowned Chicken Man. I decided to try and save my life. I wasn't sure which direction to swim. I wanted to go toward Hogboro. I wasn't sure I could make the twelve or fifteen miles, but I had to try. It really didn't matter what part of the lake I drowned in. I might as well start swimming and hope for the best.

I struck out. I hadn't gone ten yards when something grabbed me by the ankle and pulled me under.

13

I kicked and struggled, but whatever had me by the ankle was stronger than I was. I could have looked down and seen what had got hold of me, but I was too scared. There are some pretty big fish and turtles in Lake Mishagoo. Besides, I couldn't take my eyes off the light coming down from the surface. It was getting farther and farther away as I went down into the darkness. My lungs hurt . . . I wanted air . . . I wanted to live . . . I wanted Mom and Dad.

All of a sudden, I was going up toward the light like a cork. Whatever had hold of my ankle had let go. I was kicking like mad. I burst out of the water into the sunlight. I gulped air. I turned and floated on my back. I was so glad to be alive that I almost forgot about being fifteen miles from shore and sure to drown. I looked into the blue sky.

"Victor, you must be crazy. You hire a guide, and then you don't do one damn thing he tells you." It was Charlie. As I spun around to see where his voice was coming from, my feet touched bottom. We were standing in shallow water. There was a beach and trees about a hundred yards off.

"I had to dive back under the barrier and drag you here," Charlie said. "You were starting off for Hogboro without so much as a fare-thee-well, you maniac!" Charlie was telling *me* that *I* was crazy.

I was about to say something about that when I remembered that there *was* an island, that I was standing on the bottom, and that Claudia was paddling around, looking mad as a wet hen, which she was. "I'm sorry," I said. "I guess I panicked."

"No need to apologize," Charlie said. "It's all in a day's work for a licensed guide. Now let's get on shore and get our clothes on. They'll be coming to meet us soon."

We walked through the shallow water to the beach. Beyond the beach there were a lot of tall trees with silvery trunks. We got into our clothes. Claudia was walking around and sort of shaking herself and muttering.

"There should be some lizards along to meet us any minute," Charlie said. "We'd better wait on the beach—there may be wild pigeons in the woods."

"How are the lizards going to know we're here?" I asked. "We didn't make a lot of noise, or tell them to expect us, or anything like that. And what does it matter if there are pigeons in the woods?"

"First of all, the lizards know that we're here, you can be sure of that. There's very little happens on this island that the lizards don't know about. As for the pigeons, there goes one now." Charlie pointed to a perfectly ordinary pigeon flying overhead. That is, it seemed perfectly ordinary until it came down a few hundred feet and I could see it was as big as a horse. Claudia growled.

"Can those things hurt us?" I asked Charlie.

"Do you want to find out?" Charlie said.

"No—but—I mean, you've been here before—"

"Who has?" he asked.

"But you know all about how to get here, and the lizards, and the big pigeons—how'd you find out all that stuff?"

Charlie tilted his head toward the chicken.

"Claudia?" I said. "Claudia told you about all this?"

"You really ought to get to know Claudia," Charlie said. "She's a very interesting bird—been everywhere—knows things." Claudia was watching the big pigeons flying away in the distance and sort of snarling.

You'd think it would be sort of a shock to meet lizards that walk on their hind legs and stand about five feet tall. I mean, even after seeing them on television, it would have to be a little strange to meet them face to face. But something had been happening over the past few days. I was getting more and more used to the way lizards looked, their expressions and all. They seemed pretty human-looking, and I wasn't too upset by the appearance of the lizards who came to meet us. There were maybe a dozen of them. They came out of the trees, walking easily on their hind legs. They

93

walked toward us. It was eerie—the green lizards and the silvery trees. The sand was yellow, and the sky and water were deep blue. It was like a dream. I mean, it was really happening—I knew that—but it was so vivid, the focus was so sharp, and there didn't seem to be any sound. The lizards walked silently, the lake was silent, even Claudia had shut up—and I don't even remember hearing myself breathe.

"Five-men!" the lizards said. "Five-men—like us!" They were looking at our hands.

"Isn't Fergussen with you?" one of the lizards asked.

It was the first time I had ever seen Charlie look surprised. "How do you know about Fergussen?" he asked.

"You're the Chicken Man, aren't you?" a lizard asked. "And that's Claudia, and that's Victor, right?"

"How did you know that?" Charlie asked. He really looked funny. He was sort of gasping and working his eyebrows.

"We saw you on televison," one of the lizards said. "You're the most popular show in town. We've been watching you for weeks. Everybody especially likes it when Shane Fergussen makes chocolate sodas for Claudia."

Charlie whispered to me. "They've been watching us while we're watching them. Their television must work differently."

"How rude of me not to introduce myself," the lizard who had been doing all the talking said. "I am

Reynold, and these are my friends, Reynold, Reynold, Reynold, Reynold, Reynold, Reynold, Reynold, Reynold, Reynold, Reynold, and Reynold."

"Is everybody here called Reynold?" I asked.

"Of course not," Reynold said. "That would be ridiculous. There are lizards named Raymond and Helena and a lot of things."

While we were talking with the lizards we had begun to walk. It was soundless walking, the way the lizards had walked when I first saw them. I was doing it too. I know that walking on a sandy beach doesn't make any noise, but this was even quieter. Usually you can hear *some* sound—sand shifting, your own breathing, someone else's breathing, your clothes rustling, something clinking in your pocket—but this walking was without a sound. We walked through the silvery trees. The floor of the forest was sandy. We walked without saying anything. Sometimes the lizards were ahead of us, sometimes they were behind us. Claudia was sitting on Charlie's shoulder with her head tucked under her wing.

We came to a hilly place in the forest. The trees were thicker. Streams ran through the forest, sometimes at the bottom of deep channels. There was a good smell. It wasn't a regular forest smell; it was spicy, like cookies at Christmastime. Once or twice I thought I heard music—lizard music in the distance. We walked for a long time and fairly fast. I never got tired. The cool, spicy air made me feel very wide awake. We had been going up and downhill for some time, but mostly uphill. The sky was turning yellow. The leaves on the trees were getting less green and taking on a pale blue color. The spice smell was very strong. It made me hungry and made me feel as though I had just eaten something nice, both at once. The sand was a very bright yellow color, like gold. Still silence. Still going fast. Still going uphill mostly. It was the best walk I've ever taken in my life. There were times when I didn't notice anything about the air and the trees and the yellow sky. I just felt the pleasure of moving, just walking. It was so easy. Walking can be wonderful. I didn't have a thought in my head. I wasn't curious about where we were going. I didn't care if we never got anywhere, just walked and walked through the beautiful forest, day and night forever. I really never dreamed there was so much to walking. Other times I studied the shapes of leaves and the colors of things and what the shadows did as we passed through them. Even when I wasn't thinking, I was taking everything in. If I knew how to draw, I could draw a picture of every single leaf and tree and grain of sand that I passed on that walk. I could count the leaves in my picture, and then go back to the spot—no, more leaves would have grown. I could take a photograph that was made that day and count the leaves in the photograph, and every leaf that was in the photograph would be in my drawing. If you really look at something, really really look at it—not staring, or trying to memorize it, or anything—just look at it easily, but really look like I was doing on that walk, you will never forget even the smallest detail of what you've seen. I learned that in the forest.

After a while, it became obvious that we were climbing a mountain. Things were getting steeper and steeper, and whenever I looked back, I looked down. I really liked being high up. I never had been that high before. There aren't any hills at all where I live. In fact, the city of Hogboro built a hill in the city park so kids would know what one looked like. Sometimes I could see over the tops of the trees, all the way to the beach and the lake. The forest was getting thinner, and the soil was starting to get rocky. Sometimes I had to use my hands to get over big rocks. Of course, the lizards just skittered over the rocks when they went on all fours. They were so fast, you could hardly see them. Soon there weren't any more trees, just rocks. I could see almost the whole island. When it got really steep, a lizard would give me a push from behind, or dangle a tail for me to hold onto. There were clouds around us. Sometimes we could look down at a cloud. The rocks were a grayish blue color, some of them were green. We went up and up, it seemed like forever. I was starting to get just a little bit tired.

"We'll take a rest up there, Victor." It was Reynold who spoke—the first Reynold, the one who spoke to us on the beach. Now this is sort of funny. Even though all the lizards were named Reynold—and of course they looked pretty much identical—I could always tell which was which. Later, when I talked to a bunch of lizards named Reynold, if I were to say "Reynold," only the one I meant would respond. I mean, it worked, talking to the lizards. I always knew which one I was talking to, and they always knew too.

The place Reynold had pointed out was a little patch of grass at the very top of this big mountain. There were some big smooth rocks and a sort of thing like a tent without sides—just a roof. It turned out to be made of gold. We all sat down under the gold roof supported by wooden poles and cooled off. Someone had left some baskets there. They were perfectly round, a little bigger than basketballs, with handles on top. Reynold (another one) opened them and handed around something between cakes and cookies. They didn't taste exactly like anything I'd ever eaten and they tasted a little like everything I'd ever eaten, all at the same time. They were very interesting. I had two. There were also bottles of something like very good lemonade, only not made with lemons. It is the only stuff I ever drank that is, without a doubt, better than grape soda.

Reynold (the first one) explained to us that we were not on top of a mountain. Actually, we were on the edge of the crater of a big volcano. We could almost see that. The ridge curved away from us in both directions, making part of a big circle. We couldn't see the whole circle or down into the crater because there were a lot of clouds. The lizards were planning to take us down into the crater (the volcano wasn't active), and inside the crater was the main city of the island, Thunderbolt City. The name of the whole island was Diamond

Hard. Diamond Hard is a translation. The name in their language sounds something like *Neebleninn,* which is sort of squeaked in a very high-pitched voice with a sort of rush of air. The lizards have a very weird language. About this time, Charlie brought up the question of how come the lizards all speak English.

Reynold (another one) explained. When humans invented television, the lizards started picking it up on their sets. They had television a long time before we did. Human television became very popular with the lizards; they did almost nothing but watch it for the first few years. As I said before, they can receive not only the programs but the people watching the programs—and they can watch hundreds or even thousands of "shows" at once. It's a whole different system. Their sets are big cylinders, maybe six feet high and two feet across, and they spin. There's a sort of pin running down through the center of the cylinder, and it is held top and bottom by a frame of some kind of black stone. When a lizard wants to watch television, he gives the cylinder a spin, and it will keep spinning for hours. Little blue sparks appear at both ends of the cylinder. I know I'm not explaining this very well, but I really don't understand it. Anyway, they watch television with their eyes closed. They just sit in the room with the spinning cylinder and close their eyes and see all the shows on TV and all the people watching the shows—all at once! When human television got popular, all the lizards started speaking English. They had known about it from radio for a long time, and some lizards spoke it, but when TV came along, it got to be a sort of fad. All the lizards loved Groucho Marx and Walter Cronkite—it was the moustaches that they liked, Reynold said. I was really glad to know that someone beside me appreciated Walter Cronkite.

It was pleasant sitting under the golden roof, having the nice lizards snacks and listening to Reynold explain things about Diamond Hard and the lizards. All the Reynolds were very nice to us and kept asking us if they could get us anything and were we comfortable. But the one they were really nice to was Claudia. I mean, they just kept hovering around her and sort of smiling at her. I mean, lizards don't actually smile, but they looked at her in a sort of pleasant way. It seemed as though the lizards were happy to have us visit them, but they were really thrilled that Claudia was with them. Claudia seemed to be enjoying herself. Her feathers had dried, and she was sort of showing off, chickenlike—fluffing her feathers and clucking and tilting her head to one side. The lizards took it all in. Whenever she took a drink of the lemonade stuff or ate some of the cake crumbs, they would get all excited and look at each other and say things in lizard talk. That was about the only time I heard the lizards speak their own language—when they were excited. The rest of the time they all spoke English, even little kids. I supposed they had never seen a chicken and that's why they were so excited, but it turned out to be something else.

Coming down the inside of the crater was not easy. The clouds, once you got into them, were just fog—wet and dark and hard to see through. The rocks were wet and slippery. I didn't like it. The lizards didn't have any trouble, of course, and they sort of crowded around us and kept us from falling. Still, it was slow and wet and unpleasant. It must have taken us an hour to come down out of the clouds.

14

Reynold (the first one) told me that nobody ever forgets his first look at Thunderbolt City from high on the crater slopes. I can understand that. All of a sudden we were beneath the clouds that usually fill the mouth of the volcano. Over our heads, stretching away for miles, was a ceiling of lumpy gray—the bottom of the clouds. There was gold and white light behind the cloud lumps, and the whole thing sort of glowed. Below us was a valley, so green you can't imagine it. At the bottom was a plain, or flat place—it looked like a huge lawn—with streams and lakes that reflected gold and white. In the very middle of the big flat place was Thunderbolt City. All the roofs were made of gold. There seemed to be a hole—actually five holes—in the cloud roof over the city, and five broad rays of golden light fell on the roofs of the city. They were so bright, it was almost like staring at a hundred watt bulb. The walls of the houses were white, and they were all sort of clustered together around some big buildings like apartment houses, also with white walls and golden roofs, that stood in the center. I could see green gardens with white walls around them and green parks and ponds in Thunderbolt City. I have not mentioned this before, but I was in Disneyland once. Compared to Thunderbolt City, Disneyland is like a broken-down hamburger stand.

The path down the inside of the crater was easy after we got out of the clouds. The path was marked with white stones, and sometimes there were steps made of stone or cut from the rock of the crater wall. As we got lower, we passed little flat places cut back into the slope—squares about as big as an average back yard. Lizard farmers were working in those spaces. They all waved to us and said hello. A lot of them knew my name. They all knew Charlie—they called him Chicken Man—and they all knew Claudia. I asked Reynold (another one) why the farms were up on the slope instead of down on the flat part of the crater. He said that there were farms on the crater floor too, but certain crops grew better higher up.

Around the edge of the crater floor we came to the first lizard houses. They were farmers' houses, made of stone and painted white. The farmers and their families lived in the houses, and climbed up the crater wall every day to work the tiny farm plots. Each farmhouse was tidy and small, with a wooden roof painted yellow. Many of the farmhouses had a chicken painted over the door. I asked

Reynold (another one) about that. He said it was an old lizard custom. It was interesting, because there were no chickens on Diamond Hard. Nobody had ever seen one until humans invented TV. And yet, the custom of painting chickens on farmhouses was hundreds of years old. Reynold (the same one) guessed that there must have been chickens on the island at one time, and that's when the custom got started. That sort of explained why Claudia was such a celebrity.

By the time we had reached the farmhouses, we were walking on the flat crater floor and we could see Thunderbolt City in the distance. It was just as beautiful seen from below as it was when we looked down on it from the crater wall. The city was built on a sort of hill, right in the middle of the crater floor, with the biggest, tallest buildings in the center of town. It was getting to be late afternoon, and the sun was hitting the city at an angle. A big part of the crater floor was in shadow, and the city was shining with a slightly reddish color. What had looked like green lawns from above turned out to be fields of crops, mostly a green cabbage-looking thing about as big as a baseball that grew by the millions all along our walk to Thunderbolt City.

The shadow on the crater floor had reached the city when we passed through the Chicken Gate. There isn't any wall around the city, just a gate. The road passes through it. The gate is a huge boulder with a sort of rough door through it. It's just a natural boulder, sort of egg-shaped with this hole through it. It isn't fancy at all, except there's a golden chicken on top. The door is so low that you have to crawl through.

We entered the city. In a way, it was the neatest place I'd ever been. I mean, it was very tidy—more so than McDonaldsville. There wasn't a speck of dirt anywhere, and everything sort of just fit together. At the same time, it wasn't boring and all the same like McDonaldsville. It was busy and interesting like Hogboro. A very unpodlike place. Very lizardy. Lizards were hurrying everywhere. Many of them said hello to us, and stopped for a second to say they were glad we'd come. Then they would excuse themselves and hurry off. They were on their way home from work and school. It was lizard rush hour! Reynold explained that everybody was hurrying home so they would not miss the "CBS Evening News." There were no cars and buses. Everything moved by lizard power, so it wasn't a noisy rush hour. There was just a little noise of scampering and scratching as the lizards hurried home.

Reynold asked us if we'd like to come to his house to rest up and have something to eat. After that, he was going to take us to the place where visitors stay. This was the first Reynold talking. Charlie said that he didn't want to be any trouble, but Reynold said that it was a pleasure to have us and he wanted us to meet his family. Reynold's wife was named Helena, and he had three children named Raymond. They all knew who we were and were very excited about Claudia. The house was small and very nice, with polished wooden floors and white walls. There were drawings of Walter Cronkite that the three Raymonds had done, hanging near the television which I recognized from Reynold's description. Reynold showed us around the house. It was very plain; there wasn't much furniture. He said that if we wanted to wash, there was a little house in the back yard. We went out. It wasn't an outhouse; it was a regular bathroom made of stone. Some of the things in it were a little strange, because they were made for lizards. When I came back from my turn in the bathroom, Reynold and Charlie were watching television. It was about time for Roger Mudd. I guessed they were watching television. I mean, they were both sitting there with the three Raymonds, and they all had their eyes closed, and the big cylinder was spinning. Helena wasn't watching—she was in the kitchen fixing something to eat. I sat down between Charlie and Reynold, closed my eyes, and tried to watch too. It didn't work. I just sat there trying for the whole half hour—nothing. I guessed there was a trick to it. I made up my mind to ask Charlie how he did it, but I wanted to wait until we were alone. Reynold said something about how Roger Mudd would really be terrific if he grew a moustache, and we all sat down to supper.

The supper was the same as the snack we'd had on the crater rim. The little cakes are all they ever eat in Diamond Hard, not that I minded. It isn't the sort of food you're apt to get tired of, since it tastes like everything there is all at once, and one thing after another simultaneously. As I said, it's an interesting food. The lizards call the little cakes Thunderburgers. Of course, they're not in the least like hamburgers—it's just another English word they like.

It was like eating with any family. The three Raymonds talked about what had happened in school. Helena told Reynold what had happened while he was working, and Reynold told about our walk from the beach to Thunderbolt City. It turned out that all the Reynolds who had met us had started out the day before and slept in the forest so they would be sure not to miss us. I wanted to know how they knew we were coming. Reynold said they had seen it on TV. It seems that Reynold had some kind of job which included meeting visitors to Diamond Hard. Charlie wanted to know if they had many visitors. Reynold said almost none. Of course Claudia got most of the attention of the family. They all wanted to feed her, and whenever she took some food, they all laughed and carried on. Charlie whispered to me that he was afraid Claudia was going to get spoiled from all that attention.

After supper, Reynold said he would take us to the place where we were supposed to stay. We followed him out into the street. All the houses in Thunderbolt City glow in the dark. They don't exactly shine like light bulbs, they just glow slightly—enough to see where you're going. Reynold took us to the middle of town, up the hill and into one of the big buildings. We didn't see many lizards on the way.

Inside the big building, we went up a very long flight of stairs and then down a long hall. Reynold showed Charlie and me two little rooms with nothing in them but a sort of low bed; those were for Charlie and me to sleep in. Claudia was supposed to sleep in this real big room, with all kinds of beautiful oil paintings of Walter Cronkite and Thunderbolt City and beautiful rugs and statues of chickens. Charlie said that Claudia wasn't used to sleeping in a room of her own—usually she just slept in Charlie's hat turned upside down.

Charlie explained to Reynold that Claudia was used to sort of depending on him, Charlie, and she might not be too comfortable spending the first night in a strange place all alone. Reynold said he understood, and it was fine with him if Charlie wanted to stay in the big room with Claudia. Then he asked us if there was anything else we needed—there wasn't. Reynold said good night and left.

Charlie and I had a long talk. I wanted to know a whole lot of things about the island and the lizards. I hadn't asked too many questions of Reynold and the other lizards because I didn't want to bother anybody—they were all being so nice to us. Also, it was becoming very clear that I wasn't very important to them, even Charlie wasn't. The one they were really interested in was Claudia. She was like visiting royalty or something. It obviously had to do with all the chicken pictures and statues all over the place. I asked Charlie if the chicken was like a god on Diamond Hard. He said he didn't know—Claudia hadn't told him all that much about the place. That was something else I'd been meaning to ask him about—I had never heard Claudia say a word. I also wanted to know if Charlie had really been watching television with Reynold, or if he was just faking it like I was. I didn't get answers to any of this, because he started shushing me. He said that Claudia was getting sleepy, and we'd have to continue our talk in the morning. He pushed me out of the big room and closed the door very softly. There really wasn't any question that Charlie was very fond of Claudia and tried to make her comfortable whenever he could. I went back to my little room and fell asleep with all my clothes on.

15

"**G**ood morning," the lizard said. "My name is Reynold." He wasn't any of the Reynolds I had met the day before. "I will show you where you can wash." He took me down the stairs and led me into a sort of back yard, where there were a number of stone washrooms. Reynold waited for me. When I came out he said, "I'll take you to your friends. We can have breakfast while I tell you the plans we've made for you."

We walked back into the building where I had slept. In a large room I found Charlie and Claudia already having breakfast, those Thunderburgers again. The night before they had tasted a little like meatloaf; now they tasted a little like bacon and eggs.

"I've been telling your friends something about our island and what we'd like to show you," Reynold said. "There's a lot to see. I've made up schedules. We'll have to skip a lot, because you're going to have to leave late tonight."

I must have looked surprised, because Reynold said, "Please don't be offended—we'd love to have you stay longer. The reason we will send you off tonight is so that you will be able to get home at all. You know this is a floating island. Of course we can't control when or where it will move, but we can predict it. At high tide tonight we'll start moving, and by morning we'll be a hundred miles away."

Charlie asked a question. "Why doesn't this island ever float closer to shore than ten or fifteen miles?"

"It's the invisible wall," Reynold said, "the same thing that keeps boats from bumping into us. It's like a big invisible bumper all around the island."

Reynold took a sheet of folded paper out of his pocket. This shocked me, because he wasn't wearing any clothes. They aren't put together in the regular lizard way. Reynold unfolded the sheet of paper.

"In order to cover most of the important sights on the island, we will divide into two groups," Reynold said. He was reading from the sheet of paper. "The Chicken Man and Claudia will visit the House of Ideas and the House of the Egg. Victor will visit the House of Plants and the House of Memory. I'm afraid that's really all we'll have time for in just one day." Reynold folded up the sheet of paper. I watched to see if he was going to put it back in his pocket—I wanted to be sure I had really seen it the first time—but he just left it on the table.

Another lizard came into the room. "This is Reynold," Reynold said. "Reynold will guide Victor, while I, Reynold, will guide the Chicken Man and Claudia. To save time and give each visitor the widest possible impression of the important things on our island, Reynold will tell Victor all about the House of Ideas and the House of the Egg while they are on their way to the House of Plants and the House of Memory. Meanwhile, I, Reynold, will tell the Chicken Man and Claudia all about the House of Plants and the House of Memory while we are on our way to the House of Ideas and the House of the Egg."

The lizards seemed to be really having a lot of fun being tour guides. They were very organized and businesslike. Both of them were wearing what looked like wristwatches, but on a closer look they turned out to be flat pebbles taped to their wrists. Reynold looked at his pebble. "It's 7:15, time we started out."

Reynold and I had a fairly long walk down the hill and through the city. While we walked he told me about the places I would not have time enough to see. The House of Ideas and the House of the Egg were near the center of the city, in two of the big buildings we had admired from the plain. The House of Ideas was a big empty building with nothing in it. It had no windows and only one door. Outside the door a lizard sat at a small desk. On the desk was a little wooden box. If a lizard had an idea, he could go to the House of Ideas and give an Agama Dollar to the lizard at the desk. Then the lizard at the desk would unlock the door for the lizard with the idea, who would slip inside and shout his idea. For example, a lizard might get the idea that lizards should not give advice to their friends unless they were asked for it. He would go to the House of Ideas, pay one Agama Dollar, and shout, "Lizards should not give advice to their friends unless the friends ask for it." Then the lizard at the desk would lock the door, and the lizard who had the idea would go away satisfied.

"In this way," Reynold explained, "we have collected and kept safe all our ideas for generations."

"You mean that you think all those ideas are still in there?" I asked.

"Of course," Reynold said. "How are they going to get out?" This struck me as a little dumb, but it didn't seem polite to say anything about it.

The House of the Egg was apparently a place where they kept this egg that was sort of sacred. It seems that someone named Reynold (what else?) had been a big deal on Diamond Hard a long time ago. He invented the House of Ideas and the House of Memory and television, and all sorts of stuff. He was almost like a god to the lizards. When Reynold the first had died or gone away—Reynold (my Reynold) didn't make it clear which—he left this egg and told the lizards that one day a stranger would come to the island and the egg would hatch, and they would have a leader and do all sorts of good things—conquer the pods and everything. I stopped Reynold there. I wanted to know what he

113

knew about the pod people. It turned out that the lizards all believed in pod people. They thought that almost everybody outside Diamond Hard was a pod.

"Lizards and pods are natural enemies," Reynold said. I had sort of figured that out for myself. Anyway, when the egg hatched, the lizards would start to fulfill their destiny, as Reynold put it. They would become a powerful influence in the world outside, everybody would see their television programs, the House of Ideas would be broken open, and all the good ideas would flood out into the world, and it would be the end of podism. It was all going to start with a visitor to the island, and that's why they had everything ready for visitors and were so nice to them, even though nobody ever found their way to the island for years at a time. They never knew when it would be the visitor who would hatch the egg.

I guessed the egg, if it really was still hatchable, had some kind of baby super-lizard in it, maybe like a crocodile or a dinosaur. Reynold told me that when the egg was hatched, the invisible barrier around Diamond Hard would start breaking down, so everybody could come to Thunderbolt City and enjoy the House of Plants and the House of Memory.

It all made a good story (maybe it was even true), but I hardly thought Diamond Hard would get to be a big tourist attraction because of the House of Plants and the House of Memory—not if they were no more interesting than the two places where

114

Charlie and Claudia were being taken. After all, one was just a big empty building, and the other one was just a place with an egg in it. I didn't see how those things could be very interesting. I mean, Diamond Hard has a lot of wonderful stuff, and I think anybody would enjoy a vacation there, but looking at monuments is always a bore. Whenever I go someplace with my family, they always stop and read those signs along the road: In 1852 So-and-So Stole A Cow on This Spot. And it is just a spot with a few trees maybe. I guess maybe my family would like to go and see the egg.

It turned out that the House of Plants was very interesting after all. I really wasn't prepared for that after the description of the House of Ideas and the House of the Egg. The House of Plants was a big greenhouse all made of glass. It was hot and muggy inside and raining in places. It was like a jungle. There were all sorts of weird plants and trees. Some of them looked like nothing I had ever seen before. There was a Diamond Tree—that's its name. It had a trunk as clear as glass, and the leaves and branches were transparent too. It shimmered like diamonds and reflected rainbows of light. Yet if you touched the leaves and branches they bent. They looked as though they should have been brittle. There were trees with bright blue leaves and red trunks. There were plants that moved con-tinually—like dancers. There was something called the Truth Tree. It was a sort of dumpy, scruffy, dark green thing like a bush or shrub. It didn't have much of a shape, and the leaves were moldy-looking.

"This is the most beautiful plant here," Reynold said. "Don't you think so?"

"Yes, it's very nice," I said, trying to be polite.

The Truth Tree shook its leaves and made a noise. *BRRRRATT!*

"You lied," Reynold said. "It does that whenever anyone lies." He was laughing.

"Why didn't it do that when you said it was beautiful?" I asked.

"Because I really believe it," Reynold said.

Truth Trees are planted in all the front yards in Thunderbolt City. Before a lizard takes an idea to the House of Ideas, he tries it out on the Truth Trees. There were other trees and plants; almost all of them had something special about them. The House of Plants was the most fantastic place I'd ever seen. When Reynold told me that it was time to leave, I didn't want to go. I was starting to feel that all the plants were my friends. I mean, it was like the Hogboro Zoo only much better. Reynold insisted. It was time to go to the House of Memory. We had to keep up with the schedule.

16

There had been lizards strolling inside the House of Plants, and lots of lizards watering and taking care of the plants. Outside, lizard families were having picnics, and lizard kids were playing ball. The whole place had the atmosphere of a park or a zoo.

The House of Memory was a very different sort of thing. We took a narrow path that started behind the House of Plants. There was tall grass on both sides, and the path was dusty. It wound down through taller and taller grass. The grass was spiky. Mosquitoes buzzed around us, and I got a lot of bites. The path kept going downward. There were some scraggly trees and bushes with stickers. We were getting into a forest, a dark one. It wasn't like the forest we had passed through on the slopes of Diamond Hard. This forest was sort of mean and dark and mosquitoey. My nose was full of dust from the path. I was hot and sweaty, and sort of scared. I

117

really wished we could have stayed in the House of Plants. I wished it even more when I saw the House of Memory.

It was a little hut made of sticks and bundles of grass. There was a little dirt clearing around it, and there were lots of mosquitoes all around. The whole thing wasn't any bigger than maybe a couple of telephone booths.

"This is the House of Memory," Reynold said. "I'll wait outside for you." It was obvious that both of us wouldn't fit inside very well. There was a little low door, like the door of a doghouse. It was dark inside, and there was a sort of sweet hay smell that I didn't like.

"What's inside?" I asked.

"You have to see for yourself," Reynold said, "and don't think about a snake." I hadn't been thinking about a snake! Up until then, I hadn't. Now I couldn't think of anything else. This whole thing scared me. I really didn't want to go inside the hut. There was a sort of watermelon smell that was making me nervous.

"I don't want to go in there," I said.

"You have to go in," Reynold said. "It's on the schedule."

I didn't want to make a fuss. All the lizards had been so nice to me. I figured it wouldn't take more than a minute to look at everything inside the hut and come right out again. It seemed very important to Reynold, and he showed no sign of letting me get away without seeing whatever was inside the House of Memory. What had he meant about

118

snakes? Why shouldn't I think about one? And why couldn't I stop thinking about one? "It's just an old shack," I thought. I was sweating. Then Reynold did a very unfriendly thing—he just shoved me inside the hut.

It was dark inside. I couldn't see a thing. Then I saw something. It was the biggest snake I ever saw, bigger than the one in the Hogboro Zoo, and he was standing up and looking me in the eye, and he was a cobra.

"He can't hurt you!" Reynold shouted from outside. "I told you not to think about a snake!"

I can say for sure that I have never been so scared in my life. I just stood there with my knees shaking. I wanted to run, but I was afraid to move. By the way, the cobra was white. That made it worse. For the second time in two days, this time for real, I was sure I was going to die.

"Think about a corn muffin!" Reynold shouted, and the snake turned into a corn muffin. I looked at the corn muffin, a regular corn muffin. I thought about the snake. The corn muffin started to wiggle a little. I thought about a corn muffin—it was still. So that was how this place worked! You had to be careful what you thought about. I didn't like it. I made for the door. But the door wasn't there. This may sound funny, but the House of Memory was much bigger on the inside than on the outside. I mean, a whole lot bigger. It was as big as a barn at least, maybe as big as a football field. It was fairly dark, but there was enough light to make my way around. I guessed the light was coming from the

119

doorway, and I tried to make my way in that direction.

"What is this place supposed to be?" I thought. I really didn't like it. Then I found the squirrel. It was my old gray squirrel. Not a real one, the one I had as a little tiny kid. This squirrel really meant a lot to me when I was a baby, and I was happy to see it again. It wasn't just a squirrel like mine, it was the same one. I mean, I used to know every inch of that squirrel, the places where I had sort of sucked the fur off the ears and the green thread where Mom fixed it when the stuffing started to come out. It had one original glass eye and one coat button. This squirrel was really broken in, and there wasn't another one like it in the world. Somewhere along the way my squirrel had disappeared. I never did know what happened to it. To tell the truth, a month didn't go by when I didn't wonder what happened to my squirrel. Finding it like that really made me feel good. When I picked it up, all the old feelings came back—not that I go around sucking the ears of stuffed animals. It just felt and smelled the way I remembered it. The House of Memory! So that was what this was! I walked around in the almost darkness, holding my squirrel by the hand, to see what other memories I could find.

There were a lot of them. It was like walking around in a store or a museum. I recognized a few memories of mine, mostly baby stuff—my little bowl, my blue blanket, stuff like that. There were a lot of baby bowls that I didn't recognize too, other people's memories. There were memories that were really strange. I think they might have been memories of animals, or even plants and rocks— funny things like sounds, warmth, reddish light. My squirrel and I walked around among all the memories, looking for pretty or interesting ones. Little girls' party dresses were popular, also scenes of the insides of rooms. There were no people. I don't know why, maybe the lizards don't collect those. Some of the strangest memories were feelings. You are walking along, and all of a sudden you are in a big puddle of warmth, or fear, or anger, or pleasure, or a particular smell. Then you step out of it and you're back in the dark looking at some- body's cap-pistol. I noticed that the majority of the memories were kid memories. There weren't many grownup things. Also, you can pick up and handle your own memories, but other people's memories are just like shadows. You can put your hand right through them. The one I really liked was a bunch of lions, maybe twenty of them, playing in this grassy place with bright sunlight. They were really great. I could smell the lions and the grass and feel the warmth of the sun. They raced around and knocked each other down and jumped each other, and wrestled, and swatted each other. They were big lions, but they weren't all grown up. I really liked looking at them. I was really close to them, almost in among them. They were really enjoying them- selves, and so was I.

I must have watched the lions for an hour. I was sitting in the grass with my squirrel, just sort of relaxing. Sometimes the lions stopped their game and all fell asleep for a while—catnaps. Then they would start up again. Lions are really nice-looking animals. After a while, I thought I could hear Reynold calling me. I got up and started walking toward the sound of his voice. After a while, I could see the doorway glowing in the distance. Reynold called me about every five minutes. I got closer. The cobra was back in the doorway. I turned him into a corn muffin. Then I thought about a cobra with a bag over his head, and he turned into that. I walked right past him and out into the sunlight.

Reynold was waiting for me, sitting on the ground in front of the House of Memory swatting mosquitoes. "Did you have an interesting time?" he asked.

"Very," I said. "How does that place work?"

"I have no idea," Reynold said. "We discovered the spot a long time ago and built the hut around it to keep people from stumbling in by accident."

"Is the snake always there?" I wanted to know.

"Search me," Reynold said.

I guessed it must be afternoon. I checked my watch—I had forgotten to wind it. I asked Reynold for the time.

He looked at his pebble. "It's 4:37." I set my watch.

"By the way," I asked, "how does that thing work?"

"What, the pebble?" Reynold asked. "It doesn't work. We wear them to show off for visitors. Most lizards just guess about the time." I put my watch in my pocket.

"We'd better start back to Thunderbolt City," Reynold said. "You're scheduled to attend a banquet with your friends and a lot of important lizards. Then we have to make preparations to send you back to Hogboro."

Reynold and I started walking up the path toward the House of Plants. "Did the House of Plants get started like the House of Memory?" I asked.

"That's right," Reynold said, "we just found all the plants there and built the greenhouse to protect them. Probably Reynold planted them." He meant Reynold, the old-time hero who started everything on the island.

When we reached the House of Plants, Reynold bought us Thunderburgers and cups of tea from a little stand outside the greenhouse. I saw him give the lizard two Agama Dollars, but I didn't manage to catch him putting his hand into his pocket, or taking it out. We sat on a bench and ate our Thunderburgers. This time they tasted a little like flowers. Then we drank the tea, which was bitter, and started walking back to the city. We were halfway there when I realized that I had left my squirrel in the House of Memory.

There was a big commotion going on when we reached Thunderbolt City. Lizards were running everywhere. I couldn't find out what was going on because they were all talking in lizard. I tried to ask Reynold what it was all about, but he had become so excited that he forgot to speak to me in English. He just kept repeating the same thing over and over

123

in lizard talk. Reynold started running, and I ran with him.

There was a big crowd in the middle of Thunderbolt City. The lizard band that I had seen on TV was on the roof of a building playing. Lizards were cheering and dancing. Lots of the lizards were holding statues and pictures of chickens over their heads. There were thousands of lizards in a sort of open square outside the biggest building, the one with a golden egg on top. I guessed that was the House of the Egg. The lizards were really happy. I lost track of Reynold when a lizard grabbed me by the hands and started dancing with me. Then another lizard wanted to dance with me, and another one. I was in the middle of a thousand dancing lizards. They were all speaking in lizard. I had no idea what was going on. It didn't seem likely that this was a going-away party for Charlie and Claudia and me. However, the lizards did go all-out to be nice to visitors.

I noticed that the wrist of the lizard I was dancing with had a flat pebble taped to it. I looked up. It was Reynold, my guide that afternoon.

"What's going on?" I shouted.

"Neeble, neeble neeble neeble," Reynold said.

"Speak English! I don't understand you! Speak English!" I screamed. I shook him by the shoulders.

"Oh. Yes, of course. I do apologize," Reynold said. "You don't know what's happened. *Neeble neeble neeble neeble.*" He was so excited that he had slipped back into lizard talk.

"English! English!" I shouted.

124

"Oh yes. Sorry." Reynold said, "it's just that I'm so excited. You see. The egg. It's hatched!"

Reynold was really so excited that he couldn't stand still. He was sort of hopping up and down the whole time he was talking to me. Another Reynold appeared. "Victor, I've been looking for you. You have to start for the coast soon. Come along and say good-bye to your friends." He took me by the hand and started leading me through the crowd of dancing lizards.

"Good-bye? What do you mean?" I asked, but he didn't hear me over the music and the shouting.

It wasn't easy to get through the crowd. We would go a few steps in one direction, and then get swept back to where we started by the surging, swirling, dancing lizards. Everybody was patting me on the back and saying *neeble neeble neeble neeble* to me.

"*Neeble neeble neeble,*" I said back, and the lizards laughed and smiled and patted me on the back some more. I still don't know what *neeble* means. I guess it means all sorts of things, depending on how you say it. It appears to be the only word in their language.

We finally got to a little wooden side door in the House of the Egg. Reynold pounded on the door. "Open up. It's me, Reynold, and I've got Victor with me."

The door opened, and we popped inside.

17

When the door closed, the noise of the crowd shut off as though someone had turned off a TV set. The House of the Egg had thick walls.

"Come this way," Reynold said. We climbed a long flight of stone stairs. At the top of the stairs we passed through a door into a big room. It was the fanciest room I had seen in Diamond Hard. The walls were white with gold trim, and there were little plaster chickens carved on the corners of the ceiling. There were heavy red drapes tied back with gold ropes with gold tassels. In the middle of the room was a fountain made out of a greenish stone with gold running through it. In the middle of the fountain was a gold statue of Walter Cronkite. The water came out of his pipe. The floor was made of green and white stone in squares, like a checkerboard. There was a thin edge of gold around each square. There was this real fancy chandelier made out of diamonds or glass cut in the shape of eggs. It was some fancy room.

There were a lot of lizards standing around wearing black top hats. Some of them had red or white silk sashes running across their chests, and some of them had fancy medals around their necks. They were talking quietly and drinking lizard lemonade from little cups.

All the lizards in top hats shook hands with me and said, "The egg is hatched." They seemed very happy about it. Someone was just handing me a cup of lemonade, when Charlie came through a big gold door.

"Victor! Come in here and see what we've got!" Charlie said. He was wearing a top hat too, and a red sash, and a gold medal with a diamond the shape and size of an egg in it. He waved me into the room he had just come out of. It was fancier than the room with the Walter Cronkite fountain, only cozier. It was sort of like a king's bedroom. Running around on the floor was a tiny baby chick, all yellow and fuzzy, and running around after it, clucking, was Claudia.

"You can see what happened," Charlie said. "No sooner did Claudia and I come into the room where they kept the egg—you were told all about the egg, weren't you?"

I said I was. "It's supposed to hatch out the king of the lizards or something," I said.

"Something like that," Charlie went on. "Anyway, the minute we laid eyes on it, it started to make noises, clicking and so forth. Reynold got really upset and ran for the lizards whose job it has been to look after the egg all these years. Claudia's instincts took over, and she hopped on top of the thing. If she had done that when there were any lizards in the room, I don't know what would have happened. You know they're very respectful of that egg. They even put the empty shell in a vault for safekeeping. Anyway, being cold-blooded folks, they might not have really understood what Claudia was trying to do. It all worked out for the best, because by the time the egg-keeping lizards returned, the egg had just about hatched. They were going to say something about Claudia sitting on top of their sacred egg, but she gave them a look that could freeze water, and in the next second out popped a brand-new baby chick, the same one you see Claudia chasing around the room. She's a pretty old chicken, but apparently she hasn't forgotten a thing. You should have been there, Victor. The lizards didn't know what the chick was, never having seen one, and Claudia and I had to explain that it was a baby chicken. Once they understood that, they nearly went crazy. Claudia knows how they feel about chickens around here. They like them better than anything. It seems they didn't know what was supposed to hatch out, but a chicken suits them just fine."

While Charlie was talking, the door opened a couple of times, and lizards came in to see if the new baby chick king needed anything. Both times Claudia chased them out of the room.

"See, Victor," Charlie said, "what happened is this. The lizards don't know anything about raising a baby chick and they've asked Claudia to stay around a while and sort of help out. Naturally, where Claudia goes, I go. So I'll be staying on too. You, Victor, will have to go back to McDonaldsville."

"Why?" I asked. "I like it here. I'm having a good time. I want to stay on the island!"

"What about your family?" Charlie asked. "You're an exceptional kid, Victor, but still a kid, you must admit. Don't you think it is suitable for you to continue growing up in your own home?"

"No!" I said. "My own home is boring. I want to stay here and be a lizard!" I was getting pretty upset.

"Victor, we will not argue about this," Charlie said. "You know that you have to go home. Now think about it for a minute. You don't want to upset your parents, do you?" He was right of course, but I really didn't want to leave the island yet.

"Let me stay for another week. My parents are away—they won't even miss me," I said.

"The island may not come back this way for a year or more," Charlie said. "Besides, you know the legend about the egg. The island is supposed to start getting less invisible now, easier to get to. I'll see to it personally that you get back sometime. You have the Chicken Man's word of honor."

"When will I have to leave?" I asked.

"Right now," Charlie said. "They'll have a hard job getting you to the coast before the island starts moving. Transportation from the island to Hogboro is being arranged right now."

"There are a lot of things I never found out," I said. "I never found out where the lizards came from, or whether pod people really exist, or a whole lot of stuff."

"There isn't time to tell that story now," Charlie said. "I'll try to send you a letter in care of Shane Fergussen. By the way, I wouldn't tell anyone but him what happened. Anybody else might think you were nuts."

A lizard stuck his head inside the door. "The bearers are ready to take Victor to the water," he said.

"You'd better get started," Charlie said. He patted me on the back. Claudia clucked good-bye, and the lizards hustled me down the stairs to the side door.

Four lizards were waiting for me. They were carrying a big flat board, like a surfboard, on their shoulders. I was lifted by many pairs of lizard hands, plopped on top of the surfboard, and we were off. The lizards ran, carrying the board. They were pretty fast. I would say they got up to about thirty miles per hour. We headed out of the city and into the big plain that was the crater floor. Every so often I would see a lizard sitting by the roadside. When he saw us coming, he would jump up and start running in the same direction, a little slower than the lizards carrying the board. As we caught up with him, the running lizard would fall in behind one of the lizards carrying, and that lizard would drop out. This went on the whole time I was traveling overland by surfboard. No lizard carried the board for more than about fifteen minutes. When we were climbing up the inside of the crater wall, the lizards changed places maybe every five minutes, and in the really rocky places there were hundreds of lizards who didn't run, but just passed the surfboard from hand to hand. I made the whole trip at a steady speed, and at no time did the surfboard ever stop or slow down. The lizards were so skillful in handling the surfboard that it never rocked at all. I was able to sit on it as comfortably as if I were sitting on a solid floor. In fact, after I got to feeling confident, I even stood up and walked back and forth on the fast-moving board. It was quite a ride.

It was late afternoon when we reached the crater rim. I took a last look at Thunderbolt City. The red sunlight was making the gold rooftops shine. A minute later we were running down through the forest on the outside of the volcano. The lizards sort of sang or chanted as they ran with the surfboard. When a new lizard took his turn, he would join in the song.

Before long I could see the lake through the trees. The sun was almost setting, and the water was shining red and gold. The lizards put down the surfboard and told me to take off my clothes. As I undressed, the lizards put my stuff into the same garbage bag that Charlie and I had used when we came onto the island. The bag was tied around my ankle, I got back on the board, and the lizards carried it out into the water. Nobody had stopped to say good-bye to me, or shake hands, or anything.

That bothered me a little. I was sitting on the surfboard, and maybe a dozen lizards were swimming alongside. It was getting dark, and I was a little worried that they were going to get me through the barrier somehow, and just leave it to me to find my way back to Hogboro. What the lizards did when we reached the barrier was all grab hold, drag it underwater, give it a terrific shove, and the board with me hanging onto it just slid under the barrier and bobbed up on the other side.

I looked around for the island, and it was nowhere in sight. There wasn't a lizard in sight either. It was almost dark. I could already see a glow on the horizon that had to be from the lights of Hogboro. It wouldn't be too bad, paddling the surfboard to the city. I could rest on it. I wasn't in any danger of drowning. There was a loop of rope attached to the front of the board. I crawled forward to grab it. I thought I might loop it around me so there would be less chance of my falling off the board if I fell asleep. When I touched the rope it was taut. Also, when my hand touched the water, I could feel that the board was moving—fast. It was moving toward the lights of Hogboro. There was just enough light to see the ends of the rope disappearing into the water. Something under the surface was towing the board and me. It was something pretty strong too. I lay down on my stomach and held onto the sides of the board. I kept the plastic garbage bag between my feet. At the rate the board was going, it would have dragged me into the water if it fell overboard. To play safe, I should have untied it from my ankle, but I never thought of that until much later.

It was a turtle that was towing me. He took a rest after a while—came to the surface, looked around, burped, submerged, and went back to towing. He was as big as a house. Actually. He was as big as a small house. I never knew that there were turtles that big in Lake Mishagoo. I didn't get a real good look at him. All I could see was the outline of his shell between me and the lights of Hogboro. He was definitely as big as a house.

The ride couldn't have taken much more than an hour. The turtle swam under the board, bumped it over, and left me sputtering in the water about a hundred yards from shore. He and the board were gone. I could see the headlights of cars that were driving on the road that goes along the lakefront in Hogboro. I swam with the garbage bag floating behind me and crawled up onto the beach. There was a street light not far away. There was a green haze of air pollution and mosquitoes around it. I sat on the beach, drying off for a while. I felt sort of depressed. Charlie and the lizards, even the turtle, had all rushed me out of Diamond Hard as if they were throwing out the garbage. There was probably a big party going on to celebrate the new baby chick king. I wasn't going to be there. I probably wouldn't even get to see it on TV, because the island was scheduled to float away during the night.

I slowly untied the garbage bag and got my clothes out. I got dressed and started to fold up the garbage bag. There was a big wire wastepaper basket under the street light, and I thought I'd dump it there. There was a lump in the bag. I had left something in it. It felt too big to be anything but a shoe, even too big for that. Besides, I was wearing both shoes. I unfolded the bag and reached inside. There was something soft and familiar in there. It was my squirrel. There was something shiny hanging around his neck on a ribbon. It was a little gold medal with an egg-shaped diamond in it. On the back there was an engraved inscription. I ran over to the street light and read it:

TO OUR FRIEND VICTOR,
WE WILL NEVER FORGET YOU.
REYNOLD AND THE GANG.

I crossed the road carrying my squirrel, and headed for the bus terminal.

18

A couple of days later Leslie came home. She had a bad sunburn and some kind of a nasty rash. She had this cream all over her nose and was in a bad mood. The trip had ended early when the local police had fined her and her friends for camping without a permit, or starting a forest fire or something. I didn't bother to tell her what had been going on while she was away. Mom and Dad came home on schedule. They were in a much better mood than when they had left. They brought me a very nice belt with a silver buckle made by the Indians. It has a lizard on it made out of turquoise. I thought it was a very appropriate present. They haven't found out yet that Leslie went off and left me. It's only a matter of time.

Shane Fergussen hasn't heard anything from Charlie yet. He checks the TV channels late every night for a lizard broadcast, and he says he will tell me as soon as he starts receiving anything. Shane

Fergussen says he's sure we'll hear something from the Chicken Man and the lizards sooner or later. I guess he's right. About all we can do is wait.

Meanwhile I'm saving my money. I want to buy one of those yellow inflatable life rafts. Also, I'm looking around for a really intelligent chicken.

ABOUT THE AUTHOR

D. MANUS PINKWATER was born in Tennessee. He went to school, traveled all over the world, and wound up in Hoboken, New Jersey. His wife, Jill, is also an author/illustrator of books for children. Together, they operate a school for puppies called Superpuppy.

Mr. Pinkwater believes that all books, pictures, and puppies are gifts from Almighty God and should be received and appreciated, rather than written, drawn, and trained as though humans could do those things by themselves.

FROM THE SPOOKY, EERIE PEN OF JOHN BELLAIRS . . .

☐ **THE CURSE OF THE**   15540/$2.95
BLUE FIGURINE

Johnny Dixon knows a lot about ancient Egypt and curses
and evil spirits—but when he finds the blue figurine, he
actually "sees" a frightening, super-natural world. Even
his friend Professor Childermass can't help him!

☐ **THE MUMMY, THE WILL**   15498/$2.75
AND THE CRYPT

For months Johnny has been working on a riddle that
would lead to a $10,000 reward. Feeling certain that the
money is hidden somewhere in the house of a dead man,
Johnny goes into his house where a bolt of lightning
reveals to him that the house is not quite deserted . . .

☐ **THE SPELL OF THE**   15579/$2.75
SORCERER'S SKULL

Johnny Dixon is back, but this time he's not teamed up
with Dr. Childermass. That's because his friend, the Professor, has disappeared!